the News CReW

CHECKMATE

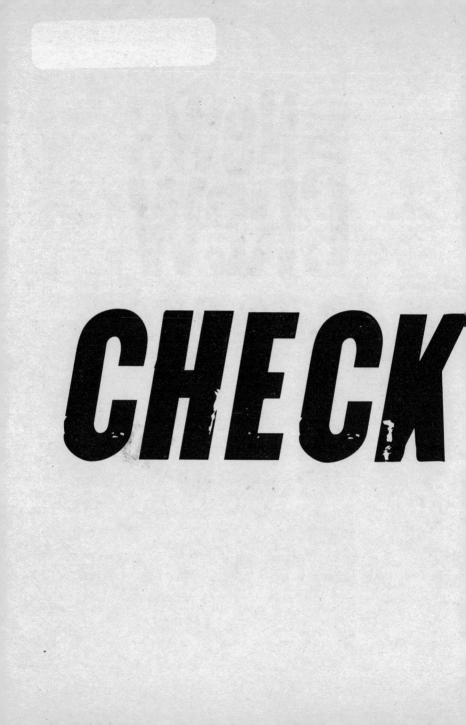

MATE

WALTER DEAN MYERS

SCHOLASTIC INC.

To Bianca

Copyright © 2011 by Walter Dean Myers

This book was originally published in hardcover by Scholastic Press in 2011.

All rights reserved. Published by Scholastic Inc., *Publishers since 1920.* SCHOLASTIC and associated logos are trademarks and/or registered trademarks of Scholastic Inc.

The publisher does not have any control over and does not assume any responsibility for author or third-party websites or their content.

No part of this publication may be reproduced, stored in a retrieval system, or transmitted in any form or by any means, electronic, mechanical, photocopying, recording, or otherwise, without written permission of the publisher. For information regarding permission, write to Scholastic Inc., Attention: Permissions Department, 557 Broadway, New York, NY 10012.

This book is a work of fiction. Names, characters, places, and incidents are either the product of the author's imagination or are used fictitiously, and any resemblance to actual persons, living or dead, business establishments, events, or locales is entirely coincidental.

ISBN 978-0-545-82875-8

10 9 8 7 6 5 4 3 2   16 17 18 19

Printed in the U.S.A. 40
First printing 2015
Originally published as *The Cruisers: Checkmate*

The text type was set in Adobe Caslon Pro.
The display type was set in Goshen and Nova.
Book design by Elizabeth Parisi and Carol Ly

CHAPTER ONE

Sidney Gets Checked!

Da Vinci Academy for the Gifted and Talented is one of those schools that's always getting experimented on. This year's major experiment was what Mrs. Maxwell, our principal (and a good lady), called the Independent Learning Project. Any kid who wanted to get extra AP credit could pick a subject, learn it on his or her own, and get the credit. The catch was that you had to convince a teacher that you really had something going on to begin the project and, after you learned whatever it was you had volunteered for, that you knew the subject well enough to deserve the extra credit. It sounded like too much work to me.

"But you will think about it, won't you, Alexander?" Mrs. Maxwell asked me.

"Yes, ma'am."

I was going to think about it, but if I could get out of it I knew I would. Anyway, a lot of kids were all gaga over the program (that's why they're at Da Vinci), and there were kids walking around school all day talking about how they were going to learn everything from Plant Biology to String Theory. It actually tired me out just hearing them.

We had basketball practice after school, and when I got home Mom was on the floor, stretching. I hoped it didn't mean she hadn't made anything for supper.

"You got a phone call," she said, reaching over to touch the heels of her hands to her toes.

"What are we having for supper?"

"I thought we could order out for Chinese food," Mom said. "Something to go along with my new job. There's a salad in the fridge if you need something right now."

"You're going to work in a Chinese restaurant?"

"Marc got me a television spot," Mom said. "They're hiring me on the strength of my demo. I don't even have to audition."

"What are you going to be doing?" I had to ask because I liked Mom working on television but I didn't want her doing underwear commercials or anything else that was sexy.

"Toothpaste," she said. "I'm going to hold up a tube of toothpaste and say why I like it. The residuals aren't that cool from Japan, but the up-front money is good. Twelve thousand bucks!"

"What's Japan got to do with it?"

"That's where the spot is going to run," she said.

"If it's going to run in Japan why are we ordering out Chinese food?"

"Because they don't have any Japanese restaurants in Harlem," Mom answered.

"That makes sense," I said. I opened the fridge and found what was left of the salad. It was mostly lettuce and tomatoes with some cheese and raisins. I passed on the salad and grabbed a can of soda. "Who called?"

"Mr. Culpepper," Mom said. "Said he wanted to talk to you about something."

Mr. Culpepper, the assistant principal of Da Vinci, didn't wear robes or anything, but I thought he could have been one of those guys in the Middle Ages who supervised torturing people. I could picture him sitting on a high stool as my ankles were being chained to the rack. I knew I hadn't done anything particularly wrong, but that didn't stop Mr. C. from being suspicious. Unless he had found out about the homework. Kambui hadn't done his essay on *The Red Badge of Courage* and had copied one from the Internet. I copied his, but I added some stuff to it so it didn't look like I copied it. I hoped.

Mom asked me what I wanted her to order from the Chinese takeout place and then got mad when I said fried chicken.

"You don't order fried chicken from a Chinese food place," she said. "You order Chinese food!"

"Then order what you want," I said.

"No, you have to tell me what you want," she said. I was in my room and she was in the doorway. "If we're going to order we might as well get what we want."

"Then how about fried chicken?"

"Why are you being mean to me?" Mom asked. "What did I do to you?"

"So how about some egg foo yong?"

"You know you don't like egg foo yong," she said. "What is wrong with you today? You're getting to be just like your father."

"Mom, we're ordering Chinese food to go along with your Japanese commercial," I said. "Like, we left authentic about ten minutes ago."

We settled on some General Tso's chicken for me and something with beef for her and steamed dumplings. She went to order and I called Kambui.

Kambui is my main man and a cool-headed dude. If Mr. Culpepper had found out about him copying the homework he wouldn't rat me out. Then I thought about Mr. C. getting Kambui on the rack and torturing him a bit to make him talk.

I dialed Kambui and his voice came on saying he wasn't home but then he answered.

"Yo, Zander, what's up?"

"I got a call from Mr. Culpepper saying he wants to talk to me," I said. "Did he find out about the paper?"

"I don't think so," Kambui came back. "Miss Ortiz said she wasn't going to tell him."

"I didn't know she could just scan it and tell it was ripped off the net," I said. "Anyway, I meant to write it myself; that should count for something."

"She said if we get a new essay in by Friday — all six pages — she'll give us a grade," Kambui said. "Otherwise we get a no-grade, and that gets averaged into our final marks."

"Six pages? It was supposed to be three," I said.

"So what you going to do, go complain to Mr. Culpepper?"

I liked *The Red Badge of Courage*, the book I was supposed to do the essay on, but six pages was definitely foul. On the other hand, I didn't want Culpepper involved. I told Kambui to hang loose while I called our assistant principal, and I would let him know if Miss Ortiz squealed on us.

Miss Ortiz was hot, maybe the best-looking teacher in the school. Her only fault was that she expected everybody to do the work she assigned all the time. English was my thing, the reason I had gotten into Da Vinci. I was supposed to be able to write, but I didn't know I was supposed to be able to write so much.

Mom had written down Mr. Culpepper's number on her appointment pad right under Marc's name. Marc was her agent and she had written *Marc — Japan — finalized — 12K — Yes!* Twelve thousand would carry us for three months even if Mom didn't get any other gigs. I liked that. I was always worried that if we got too far behind she would have to do some stupid gig with her just wearing a bra or something.

"Hello?"

It was Mr. Culpepper's daughter. I hated her.

"Hey, Caren, this is Zander," I said. "Is your father around?"

"You in trouble again?" she asked.

"That's not your business," I said. "And anyway, I don't talk to seventh-graders after three o'clock, so go find your father."

"I think I'm going to recommend to him that he gets tougher on the hoodlum element at Da Vinci," she said.

"You do that and I'll put itching powder in your training bra," I said.

"Alexander Scott, that is a sexual reference and that is not allowed at Da Vinci!" she said. "You can be *expelled* for that remark."

"Yo, Caren, you have to have boobs before it becomes a sexual reference," I said.

"So, should I tell my father what you said?" she asked softly.

"No."

"Are you sure?"

"Caren, lighten up."

"Tell me one thing and I'll go get my father," she said. "Are you going out with LaShonda?"

"No!"

"She told Tyree that you were crazy mad in love with her," Caren said.

"Caren, get your father. Wait — do you know what he wants to talk to me about?"

"He mentioned something about your impending doom," Caren said. "You know, the usual stuff. I'll get him."

Adrian Culpepper could have been a horror movie all by himself. I had never met a kid who wasn't afraid of him. He came to school every morning looking for kids who might do something to mess up the school's reputation. He didn't talk about us as students but as "Da Vinci material." After two years he still wasn't sure that I was Da Vinci material. When me and three other students formed a group we called the Cruisers and started our own alternative newspaper, it was like waving a red flag in front of Mr. Culpepper. As far as he was concerned we were just slackers looking for an easy out. But all the kids at Da Vinci were into smart, and the Cruisers were no exception. We didn't do the same kind of smart that some kids did, but we definitely weren't slackers.

"Alexander?" Mr. Culpepper's voice came on the phone.

"Yes, sir?"

"I have a problem that I don't quite know how to handle," Mr. Culpepper said. "And I was wondering if it might not be better if some students handled it. And when I thought of a student group that might be just out of the mainstream enough to deal with this particular problem I, quite naturally, thought of you and your merry little band of incorrigible miscreants. What do you call yourselves again — the Losers?"

"The Cruisers, sir."

"Ah, yes. Well, are you willing to take on another problem? You did manage to handle the school's Civil War project without too much bloodshed."

"You mean that Independent Learning thing that Mrs. Maxwell was talking about?"

I could hear Mr. Culpepper exhale over the phone. He then let out a *mmmmm*, which he does sometimes when he's thinking about how to make our lives more miserable.

"No," he said. "To put it bluntly and quite directly, one of our students was detained for attempting to buy a controlled substance. This is obviously a very serious matter for both the school and the student involved. The faculty, of course, can offer the usual guidance, but I was wondering if you and — yes, the Cruisers — could be of help."

"A controlled substance?"

"A tranquilizer that's normally only available through a prescription."

"You kidding me?"

"Mr. Scott, I do not spend my time frivolously!" Mr. Culpepper was back to roaring.

"Who?" I asked.

"I am going to give you his name, but I do so with the understanding that confidentiality is something that you understand. If Sidney has a problem — and we're not sure that he has — we would like to help him."

"Sidney Aronofsky?"

Nothing else that Mr. Culpepper said came through. Sidney Aronofsky was school chess champion and one of the best players in the city. He had even been written up in *The Village Voice*. There was no way that I could picture him buying any kind of drug. But then again, I knew Mr. Culpepper wouldn't say it if it wasn't true. Especially to somebody from the Cruisers.

THE PALETTE

As part of *The Palette*'s ongoing commentary on school activities, the Editorial Board is issuing an opinion on the new Independent Learning Project. The board feels that one logical conclusion to the project is to do away with schools entirely. We have extended an invitation to the other newspaper, *The Cruiser*, to also weigh in on this issue.

Are Schools Necessary?

The Editorial Board of *The Palette* believes that schools are necessary because they do more than teach. They provide opportunities for poorer children that would not be available otherwise. Rich people could always have private tutors. Schools also facilitate the learning process by guiding students through the curriculum and offering help to those students who need it.

Schools focus students' learning in a

meaningful way by teaching subjects that have been proven to be useful over a period of time and also by correlating the learning process and the real world (jobs!). Without this guidance, education would be a hit-or-miss proposition that would reflect and exaggerate differences between rich and poor students. Schools are, in effect, the major avenue of equal opportunity.

The Anti-School Position
By Bobbi McCall

As a practicing salmon I feel my life and sense of adventure have been seriously limited by having to swim in a school. I would like more independence and the ability to cruise anywhere I want. Also, this swimming-upstream-to-mate business is sexist and generally not to my liking.

The Editorial Board of The Palette *regrets that the* Cruiser *representative did not treat this subject matter seriously.*

CHAPTER TWO
My Mama Done Tol' Me!

What I was thinking was that something had to have happened for Sidney Aronofsky to get involved with the police or with drugs. Sidney was the straightest guy I knew at Da Vinci, and one of the brightest. When I first transferred to the school the Gifted and Talented program was just getting started. There were some thuggy butts there from the old program, and the first day two of them came up to me and put me against the wall.

"How much you going to pay us not to kill you?" one of them said. He had his hand on my neck and was trying to push my Adam's apple through the wall on the third floor.

I thought for sure I had seen the guy on the six o'clock news wearing a ski mask and holding a nine, or maybe in the zoo swinging from one of the old tires they hang in the gorilla cage. That's when I met Sidney.

"How *dare* you push him!" He stood right next to Thuggy Butt and looked him dead in the eye.

Okay, so Sidney is, like, five and a half feet tall, round from his knees up, with a big head full of curly hair. He's got blue eyes that get wide when he's excited. Also, he kind of puffs himself up, getting bigger and bigger until you think he's going to explode. It's weird but impressive.

I thought he must have been a karate expert or something to stand up to the thug holding me against the wall. Even after the guy turned and knocked him down I expected that Sidney would jump up and bust out some cool moves and some oriental-style noises.

What he did was to slowly get up off the floor, wipe his bloody nose on his sleeve, and get right back into Thuggy Butt's face.

The next time he got knocked down he stayed down.

But that's the way Sidney was. He stood up for what he believed in. He also got knocked down a lot for what he believed in, but it didn't seem to matter to him. He couldn't fight and he had stood up for me. I had to stand up for him if I could, or at least be by his side if he flamed out. I had grown a lot taller than I had been when

I first arrived at Da Vinci, and I had grown a lot inside, too. Being in the Cruisers was part of that growing.

Right after the first marking period Mr. Culpepper had picked out four kids he thought weren't trying hard enough and brought us down to his office. He said that he had also noticed that we hadn't joined any of the good-doing groups the school had. It was all about being cool and showing the world that Da Vinci Academy was turning out class A citizens. He said we should have been the Harvard of the middle school experience.

"But there are clearly exceptions!" he said, raising his voice.

The first thing he wanted us to do was to show we were into the Da Vinci experience by joining something. I said I had already formed a group and Mr. Culpepper jumped all over that. He wanted to know who was in the group except me.

"Kambui?" I said, looking at him.

Kambui nodded and, before I knew it, LaShonda and Bobbi were nodding, too. That's how the Cruisers were born. When Mr. Culpepper asked us what we did it was Bobbi who said we were going to publish an alternative newspaper.

Kambui Owens is my best friend and a really dynamite

dude. He's into photography and one day hopes to go around the world taking photographs that make a difference in people's lives. Kambui lives with his grandmother not too far from me in Harlem.

LaShonda Powell is at Da Vinci because of her ability to design clothing. I mean, she's really good. She can design clothing and she can sew. I think she's probably going to be famous one day and have her initials on handbags. She and her brother live in a group home and she has a few issues about that.

Barbara "Bobbi" McCall is quirky, the kind of person I don't know anything about but I like her a lot. Her thing is numbers. She's fascinated with anything that has numbers attached to it and she can play around with numbers and come up with stuff that looks absolutely useless but is still somehow interesting. She also plays second board on the chess team, so you kind of get the picture of what her brain must look like.

I'm Alexander Scott but my friends call me Zander. I would like to be a writer one day. My folks are divorced and my dad lives all the way out in Seattle. He's a local weatherman. My mom is a model and sometimes she gets small roles in films or television.

Mr. Culpepper liked to say that he hated faces.

"Show me a child's face and I don't know anything about him," he would say. "Show me his school record and I will tell you everything about his past, present, and future!"

The grades of the Cruisers were mostly in the just-get-by range, but the thing about the kids at Da Vinci is that we're all smart. You can almost hear the wheels clicking when we start thinking.

"The paper will be the bomb," Kambui said. "It'll be the four of us keeping it real and speaking truth to power."

Mr. Culpepper smiled. It was the kind of look that an alligator gets just before he pounces. The grades of all the kids in the room were floating around the C+ area, and he couldn't get us on that. But if we messed up with the newspaper idea, and you could tell he thought we would, he would have us.

"Well, it sounds like a plan, doesn't it?" he said. "But we will see, *won't* we?"

Mrs. Florenz Maxwell, our principal, is a saint. Where Mr. Culpepper is loud, she's quiet. When he gets excited, she is calm. Sometimes I think they work together, but I hope she really doesn't like him. I know she likes the Cruisers because she told me. So when Mr. Culpepper called the Cruisers into his office the day after he had called me at home and I saw her sitting there I felt good.

Okay, we were in the office. Mr. Culpepper shuffled through the papers he keeps around just to shuffle, then he cleared his throat and spoke.

"Sidney has been arrested for attempting to buy drugs from an undercover policeman," Mr. Culpepper said. He looked around at us carefully before going on. "He was down in Alphabet City."

Da Vinci Academy is in Harlem. Alphabet City is what they call the section where the avenues are Avenue A, Avenue B, and Avenue C. I don't know if they ran out of names or what, but everybody knew there was some drug dealing going on down there. Also, a bunch of good poetry and some great music.

"I think that since he only inquired as to the availability of drugs, and the particular amount involved is not classified as dangerous, there won't be further prosecution," Mr. Cuipepper said. "What we were hoping was that some of his peers, you people, could talk to Sidney and see if there are problems that need handling. He won't tell us anything."

"We want to do everything we can for Sidney," Mrs.

Maxwell said. "But sometimes we don't know what to do. If he has a problem at home, perhaps we can point him in the right direction before he gets into further trouble."

"What do you think, Bobbi?" Mr. Culpepper looked toward her. "You're both on the chess team, aren't you?"

"Beats me," Bobbi said. "I'm really surprised. Zander's his friend."

"Mr. Scott?" Culpepper looked in my direction.

"Sidney's okay," I said. "We'll talk to him."

"Our concern is that there is a slippery slope that has to be avoided when any drugs are involved," Mr. C. went on. "Sidney's a major asset to this school and we don't want him incapacitated."

"Or be by himself if he has a real problem," Mrs. Maxwell added quickly.

"And this won't excuse you from the IL program," Mr. Culpepper said. "Independent Learning will be the wave of the future, and Da Vinci will lead it in the city of New York."

"If I were being burned at the stake would it excuse me from any of your programs, Mr. Culpepper?" Bobbi asked.

"If you were burning yourself on school property you would be completely responsible for any damage you caused,

Miss McCall," Mr. Culpepper said. "Away from school property would give you more leeway, of course, but would not offer an excuse to be delinquent in your assignments."

"I thought so," Bobbi said.

Outside of Mr. Culpepper's office we decided to call a meeting with Sidney to talk over his problems. Everyone except LaShonda thought that was a good idea.

"It won't work," she said. "Sidney ain't stupid. He knows drugs are wack. So what are we going to say to him?"

"If we tell him how much we care about him it could make a difference," I said.

"And how much we need him on the chess team," Bobbi said. "I heard that Hunter is hiring a professional chess coach to work with their team."

"We can't do anything until we scope the problem," I said. "Let's talk to Sidney and see what's happening."

Everybody agreed to that and I was feeling good about it. Then Bobbi and LaShonda got into it again.

Me and Kambui usually take things pretty easy. The two girls, LaShonda and Bobbi, get excited about everything. LaShonda is always excited to begin with, and Bobbi, who is always smiling and always giving out her squinchy-eyed look, is not excited until you disagree with her. Then she gets mad. So when Bobbi announced that she had entered a project for the Cruisers in the Independent Learning Project and LaShonda didn't like it, the sparks began to fly.

"Yo, girl, who are you to tell all of the Cruisers what we're going to be doing?" LaShonda asked.

"Yo, girl, if you want to be into some project away from the Cruisers, just go for it," Bobbi said. "You probably can't handle the theme I put out anyway."

"I can snatch all the hair off your little round head!" LaShonda said. "And then beat your butt until you turn red, white, and blue."

"How intelligent!" Bobbi was getting up into LaShonda's face.

Kambui separated the two girls by stepping in between them.

"What is your project?" he asked Bobbi.

"Well, we have to learn one subject all on our own and prove it to a teacher," Bobbi said. "So I thought we could learn the statistical basis of basketball. I call it In-Your-Face Probability Theory."

"You can't learn no . . ." LaShonda tilted her head to one side. "You mean like what percentage of shots they make and stuff like that?"

"There are a lot of basketball stats we can use," Bobbi said. "And since the final result is numerical, there has to be some angle we can work."

"If we can get a math teacher to approve it," Kambui said.

I liked the idea of getting basketball involved in an academic program. I was also thinking it would make the Cruisers seem even cooler.

"I'm not sure, but I'll go along with it," LaShonda said.

"You know, Sidney is good in math, too," I said.

"And that can be our way of getting to talk to him without looking too stupid!" LaShonda said. "Zander, you are smart."

I knew that.

Kambui and I had History together and headed toward class. On the way he started talking about Sidney. He said nothing was going to work because people who used drugs wanted to be drug addicts.

"We don't know he's using drugs, Kambui," I said. "All we know is that he asked about how to get some."

"Zander, who doesn't know drugs are bad?" Kambui

asked. "Everybody knows that. You see crackheads lying around in the street, leaning against buildings, running around looking desperate. They know they're messed up and they all look miserable. You can't talk to them because they know everything you know already. And how's he going to play chess with his head messed up?"

He had a point.

THE CRUISER

A MODEST PROPOSAL

By Zander Scott

Most young kids don't smoke, don't like greasy food, don't drink, and don't like to sit around watching television 15 hours a day. But when they get into high school they get curious about these things and go out and try them because they think it's either cool to do them or because their friends are doing something stupid. Okay, so I propose that we make all little kids between the ages of 2 and 10 smoke at least 10 cigarettes a day, eat greasy fast food from a brown paper bag, watch television 15 hours a day no matter what's on, and maybe commit a few armed robberies. Then, when they get to be 11 and have all their bad habits perfected, we can tell them that they have a choice of what they do. By this time all the big kids will have been beating up the little kids on a regular basis. A 3-year-old who smokes all day won't be too tough to take in a fight! Then if we tell them to stop smoking, stop watching television, and take their grimy little hands out of the fast food bag they might even listen.

CHAPTER THREE

Circle of Lame

don't believe it," LaShonda said. "Sidney is too straight to be running around trying to cop no dope."

"Culpepper wouldn't make it up," Kambui said.

"Sidney plays chess down on Henry Street," Bobbi said. "I think the settlement house has a team. So that's near enough to Avenue A to make it seem real."

"I don't know why Mr. Culpepper thinks we can help him," I said. "But if the rest of you guys are down with it, I'd sure like to try."

"He's probably thinking that you should know something about drugs because you're black," Bobbi said. "I mean, he can't simply walk up to people and say, 'Hey, I notice you're black, can you deal with a drug problem?'"

"You're sick, Bobbi," I said.

"But she's probably right," LaShonda said. "But maybe, just maybe, he's not using drugs. Could be he was trying to get them for somebody else."

"You ask me and I'm thinking that what I see don't smell right," Kambui said. "Something's funny here and it's not about ha-ha!"

"We can have an intervention, like they do on television," LaShonda said. "You ever see those programs where they get somebody in a room and tell them they got to stop doing *whatever* and everybody is screaming and stuff? That's what we need to do."

That seemed like a good idea and we contacted Miss LoBretto and asked if we could use the media center. She said we could and Bobbi said she could get Sidney to come to a meeting during lunch.

"Maybe everybody shouldn't come," I said. "Sidney did me a solid when I needed it most. If I can do him one, then I got to be on time. If you want to show, then that's cool. If you don't want to show it's still cool."

"It's not that, Zander," Kambui said, shaking his head. "I got some druggies in the fam, man, and it don't go down smooth no matter how much heart you got in it. You know what I mean?"

"If it was the druggies in your fam would you be at the media center?" I asked Kambui.

"I'd be there," he said.

After school I walked home by myself. I had Sidney's phone number and thought I would call his house before he got home. His grandfather was a cool old Russian dude and he loved to talk. Maybe he would say something that would give me a clue to what was going down with Sidney. But when I called it was Sidney who answered.

"Hey, Big Sid, how you doing?"

"I've done better," was the answer.

"I heard you had a little trouble," I said.

"Zander . . . Zander . . . the cops said I was facing Juvenile and then State," he said. I could hear him crying.

"What's that mean?"

"It means I could go to juvenile jail until I'm eighteen and then get switched to a regular prison," he said. "God, man, I'm really scared. I'm really scared. I didn't think any of this would happen. I really didn't."

"Sidney, you have friends, dude. I know a lot of times they drop the cases," I said. "Guys around my way don't even worry if they're caught with drugs. They just have to go downtown, stay a few hours while they get written up, and then they're back on the street again."

"You think I can get off?" I could hardly hear him.

"Yeah, look, the Cruisers are having a meeting and we'd like to invite you."

"Other people know about this?"

"Sort of . . . but that's good," I said, thinking as fast as I could. "The important thing is to get you out of trouble. Do your parents know?"

"Yeah."

"Oh."

"They want to send me to Europe or Siberia or wherever."

He agreed to come to the meeting in the media center, but I had a funny feeling about it. In my life things don't work out that easy. I thought he would be upset when he found out that the other Cruisers knew about his problem. I wondered if he was more involved in drugs than we knew and was desperate for help.

When I got home I asked Mom if she knew anything about drugs.

"Why?" she asked.

"Just wondered."

"Did anyone offer you drugs in school?"

"Not unless you think that education is the opiate of the people," I said.

"What does that mean?"

"Nothing."

"Don't say *nothing* to me," Mom said. "I'm your mother!"

"Karl Marx said religion is the opiate of the people because he felt that religious people wouldn't rebel against the government," I said. "I just substituted education because it sounded cool."

"Go back to *nothing*," Mom said. "Anyway, what did you want to know about drugs?"

"A kid in my school was caught trying to buy some prescription drugs," I said. "But this is a real good kid and I don't think he would use drugs."

"Who?"

"Just a kid."

"Kambui?"

"Why does it have to be a black kid?" I asked.

"Did he offer you any drugs?"

"I'm sorry I asked," I said.

"That's how it starts," Mom said. "You turn away from your parents and go out on your own. The next thing you know you're experimenting with drugs."

"I'm not experimenting with drugs," I said.

"Should I call your father?"

"What would he say that you wouldn't say?" I asked.

"He's a scientist!" Mom said.

"He's a weatherman!" I said. "He doesn't even figure out what the weather is going to be. He just reads it off a screen."

"You sure?"

"That he doesn't figure out the weather? He told me he didn't."

"I mean about the drugs," she said, lowering her voice.

I knew what was going to happen next. A mama hug, then a mama kiss on the forehead, and then me saying I would never do drugs.

It all happened.

But it took the rest of the night to convince her not to call my father in Seattle, not to call the police, and not to take me to a rehabilitation center.

I dig the way I look but the thing about me is that I always look too young. I was wishing I was older or at least looked older when Sidney got to the media center. LaShonda and Bobbi had arranged the chairs in a circle, and Sidney sat in the chair that Bobbi indicated. Something bothered me again. It was a little too easy.

I had thought the whole thing out and had decided to start off by telling Sidney that we were on his side. But before I could get my mouth open LaShonda got her thing off.

"Sidney, I have figured out what is wrong with your dumb-butt self," LaShonda said. "You're just stupid. Why do you want to mess with drugs?"

Sidney looked down at his hands and shook his head slowly. "I just can't help myself," he said. "At first I just wanted to experiment a little —"

"And then you got hooked!" LaShonda said.

"I'm not hooked!" Sidney said, looking around at the Cruisers sitting in a semicircle. "Really, I'm not. I just enjoy the feeling so much."

"What feeling?" Kambui asked. "Like you're probably going to jail for the rest of your life? Is that the feeling you get?"

"It's like I'm — I'm floating away from all my troubles," Sidney said.

"You have a lot of potential," Kambui went on.

"People who have lots of potential can kill it off just like *that*!"

He made a circular motion with his hand and snapped his fingers.

"I know what you're saying is true," Sidney said. "Everything you're running down is right, and I do want to stay away from drugs, but . . ."

Sidney had his head down, his hands clasped in front of him. I really felt sorry for him.

"I think everybody should say why they don't think Sidney should use *las drogas*," LaShonda said.

"Why don't you start?" I said to LaShonda.

"It messes up your skin," LaShonda said.

Sidney nodded.

"It'll be messing up your whole life," LaShonda said. "You ever see those people nodding out on the corner? That's, like, a pitiful sight. Or maybe you like sleeping in hallways or on somebody's roof. Drugs are, like, the worst things in the world."

Sidney nodded.

"Here's a good reason to stay away from drugs," Bobbi said. She opened her notebook and took out a newspaper clipping. It was from *The Village Voice*.

SIDNEY ARONOFSKY NAMED CHESS MASTER

The 14-year-old student from the Da Vinci Academy for the Gifted and Talented was named one of only two school-age masters in New York City. Adrian Culpepper, assistant principal at Da Vinci, said that he expected the youth to be a grand master by the time he was 16. The youngster said that he loved chess "more than life."

Sidney put his hands over his face and I thought he was going to cry.

Kambui said that it would mess Sidney's family up as well as him. "If you're using drugs it gets to everybody you know," he said. "Just like we're here thinking about you and wanting to deal with you. People in your family are going to be hurt."

"You know what I'm thinking?" I asked Sidney. "I'm thinking you could have told us all these reasons yourself. So what we need to do is to see how sincere you are. I know you're strong because you stood up for me when I needed it. I know you're smart. You don't become a chess champion by being stupid. What's happening, man?"

"I was just wrong . . . just wrong." We were hearing Sidney but he had his head down and we couldn't see his face. "I feel like I let everybody down. The whole school."

"It's not even like you to be using drugs," LaShonda said. "If you don't die from an overdose you could get AIDS or something and die slow like those guys on the Public Broadcasting station. They looked terrible!"

"The important thing is what can we do to help you?" Bobbi said. "The same way that you would help us if one of us was using drugs."

"What drugs are you using?" I asked.

"I got busted looking for any kind of head medicine I could find," Sidney said. Slowly, he began to lift his head and I saw he was crying. Sidney is whiter than most white people but when he gets excited or upset he gets redder than anybody is supposed to get. "I guess I just kind of drifted into drugs and didn't realize what was happening until I was in too deep to back out."

He kept going on about how he should have been asking for some help but he didn't think it would get away from him.

"You can't always make it by yourself," LaShonda said.

Bobbi asked if Sidney's family knew about the drugs and he said they did.

"It really hurt my parents," he said.

All of a sudden the whole thing seemed like a lame reality show to me. Sidney was crying and covering his face with his fat, stubby fingers. Bobbi and LaShonda both looked like they wanted to go over and give Sidney a hug. I wanted to ask him more questions. The first thing was where he was getting any drugs and how come he had to ask somebody where to get some more. He was really upset, but I wasn't sure if he was upset about using drugs or not getting them, or maybe he was even getting them for somebody else and just taking the blame. I didn't want to come down too hard because if he was on the edge I wouldn't want to be the dude that pushed him over.

I made sure that Sidney put everybody's number on his cell phone.

"Look, man, you really got to get yourself straightened out," I said as we left the media center.

"Zander, I know," he said. "Culpepper got all over me today and told me what was going to happen if I got into trouble again."

"What did he say?"

"What he actually said was that I would get kicked off the chess team, probably suspended, and maybe even get kicked out of the school," Sidney said. "That was what was coming out of his mouth but he looked like he wanted to kill me on the spot."

"Did he say anything about seeing a doctor or anything like that?" I asked.

"He said something about talking to a psychiatrist," Sidney said. "He said that maybe I had an addictive personality like Arthur Conan Doyle, who wrote Sherlock Holmes."

"I don't know about that," I said. "But just call one of us when things get hard, okay?"

We were on the street and Sidney shook my hand when the bus pulled up to the stop. I watched him get on and felt really bad. Drug addicts were supposed to be weird-looking guys sneaking around in hoodies and looking nervous all the time, not kind of fat white guys who played great chess.

They were also supposed to look desperate. Sidney looked miserable but not desperate. Maybe that would come later.

THE CRUISER

THE RED BADGE OF COURAGE AND 50 CENT

By Kambui Owens

So Stephen Crane didn't even fight in the Civil War. In fact, he wasn't even alive during the war. He published *The Red Badge of Courage* in 1895 and if it took him two years to write the book he was writing it when he was about 22 or 23. So if everybody is saying you should write what you know, and Stephen Crane didn't know anything about fighting in a war, should we change the whole scene to write what you can imagine? We're studying this book in school way over a hundred years after it was written by a guy much younger than any of the writers that we know about today. Stephen Crane was born in New Jersey and eventually made his way into New York City, where he got a job as a reporter.

He was probably a cool dude but he didn't follow any of the rules that we learned about writing. So I think he was the first Cruiser. My man was laid-back, wrote a great war book, and checked out before he was 30.

If I write a book on war I will, like Stephen Crane, make the whole thing up because I don't want to have to get shot at for real. Which brings us to 50 Cent. Yo, he's bragging on how many times he's been shot and how hard he is, like so many of the other rappers, DJs, and what-have-yous. But I don't know if we're going to be talking about 50 Cent a hundred years from now.

Can u dig where I'm coming from?

The thing is that you don't always have to be on a real tip to get over. But you do have to know the difference between the real and the unreal, the Way and the Play, what's Game and what's Lame. Stephen Crane did *The Red Badge* from the heart and not the eyes. Can we follow him or do we have to walk the walk and talk the talk and blues dues our way to heaven? Speak to a Brother!

CHAPTER FOUR

She Eats Sushi by the Seashore

Are you going to have your clothes on?"

"Zander Scott! Yes, I'm going to have my clothes on. I can wear a snowsuit if you want me to. I'm just going to do a run-through of the commercial. And I'd like you to come to see me at work. Is that too much to ask?"

That's how I ended up in a studio on Ninth Avenue and 43rd Street. There were two couches and I sat on one of them with Marc, Mom's agent, and someone from the agency. Two guys took Mom into another room to get her ready. There was a glass panel on the wall opposite Marc and me, and through it I could see a huge blue screen.

"Is she going to be on that screen?" I asked Marc.

He shrugged. "I didn't see the script," he said. "They were still working on it yesterday."

"The screen's going to be behind her," the woman from

the agency said. "This is a wonderful account. I hope she pulls it off."

"I thought she had the job already," I said.

"We look for ongoing accounts," the woman said. "Not one-shot deals."

"She'll pull it off," Marc said. He didn't sound too confident.

We waited for another five minutes before they rolled a camera into the room. Then Mom came in, dressed in a kimono. She waved to me and I waved back.

The guy who was directing the shoot was in the room, too, and we could hear his voice through a speaker.

"Okay, let's just run it down cold," he said. "You look down at the *x* that's on the floor. Do you see it?"

"Yes," Mom replied.

"Then look up and do the lines," the director said. "Frank, you ready?"

Another voice. "Okay, one, two, three . . . whenever *she's* ready."

Mom was looking down, then she looked up with this big smile on her face.

"My husband cannot resist a great smile!" she said.

"Frank?" The director.

"Looked good," the videographer said.

"Do I see a shadow on her forehead?"

"I don't think so."

"Let's try it again."

Mom looking down. Mom looking up.

"My husband cannot resist a great smile."

"Jack, how's the audio?"

"It works for me."

"Let me see the clip," the director said. "Everybody relax."

We waited for a few minutes and the director was asking if they should shoot Mom while she was sitting and the videographer said she might be too tall for a good angle.

From somewhere another voice came through the speaker announcing that the clip was ready.

Mom moved to one side and leaned against the wall. The back wall lit up, and there was a picture of Mom with her head down. Behind her there was Ninth Avenue, with cars moving and all kinds of color going on. Mom lifted her head, and out came some Japanese!

"Miriam, how's it look out there?"

"Fabulous!"

"Looks good here, too," the director said. "It's a wrap. Thanks, Melba."

Everybody shook everybody else's hands and we left. That was it. We went down in the elevator with Marc and grabbed a taxi to go uptown.

"That was it?" I asked. "How come they didn't use a Japanese model?"

"They weren't sure if they wanted to use a black model or a Japanese-American model," Mom said. I saw the cabdriver look at Mom in the mirror. "But then the Japanese girl got sick. She has an eating disorder."

"She's too fat?"

"Too thin."

"I thought models were supposed to be skinny."

"The Japanese don't like their models too thin," Mom said. "Also, she overdid it. There's a lot of pressure on American models to be thin for high-fashion work. It's hard if you have a tendency to put on weight."

The whole gig looked easy to me.

My cell beeped. It was LaShonda texting me saying that Bobbi had texted her with a freak-out. Sidney had called Bobbi asking if he could borrow twenty-five dollars and he wouldn't tell her why he needed the money.

i think he wants to buy some you-know-what!

what chu wanna du Zman?

kidnap him and have 1 of thoz interventions like they do on tv? LaS

That might have been fun to do but I didn't like it. If we got Sidney somewhere all we were going to say to him were the same old things we had already said. Also, I knew that he could run it all down to us the same way we would run it down to him.

We got uptown, stopped at La Supermercado, and bought hamburgers, buns, and cheese. Mom was all bubbly and feeling good about herself and smiling the same smile she had on when she did the commercial.

"You look like you're going to bust out with some Japanese any minute," I said.

"You going to pay me?"

"I'm your son, Mom," I said. "I shouldn't have to pay you for a smile."

She gave me a big smile, which was a little strange because I had just seen her do her smile for money and knew she could put it on anytime she wanted. I was cool, though, and didn't say anything about it.

I called Kambui and told him what LaShonda had said.

45

"Yeah, she texted me, too," he said. "I think that sometimes you just got to let people go through what they got to go through. Druggies know they're foul, so what are you going to tell them that's going to make a difference?"

"How about that Scared Straight program?" I said. "You ever see it when they take those kids to jails and let the prisoners scare them?"

"They didn't scare some of the kids but they scared the heck out of me," Kambui said. "I think if I had the choice between going to jail and going into the army to fight I'd choose the army. At least you have a gun to protect yourself."

"If I can pull it off, will you back me?" I asked. "I can call my uncle Guy."

Guy was my mom's brother. He was my height but real big in the shoulders and chest. He worked for the police department in gang relations and Mom worried about him a lot. She said that when they were young anybody who wanted to go out with her had to ask Uncle Guy's permission.

"Then he would look them over and say yes or no."

"How did you like that?" I asked her.

"I always told him which ones to say yes to so I liked it fine," Mom told me.

I told Mom about Sidney wanting to borrow money

from Bobbi and that I wanted to call Uncle Guy to see if he could bring Sidney to a jail to scare him.

"If you think it might work," she said. "Guy's good with young people."

We found Guy's number at home and Mom called him and ran down the whole situation. Then Guy wanted to talk to me and I was ready to tell him that I thought that Sidney was a good kid and just needed help but he didn't want to hear that.

"Joe Weinstein still running the sports over there?" he asked.

"Yes." Cody Weinstein's father was a gym teacher in Da Vinci's athletic department.

"I'll talk to him and let you know," Guy said.

"Sidney's not an athlete," I said.

"Did I ask you if he was?"

"No."

"No *what*?"

"No, sir."

Hey, I'm not using drugs. It's Sidney. That's what I thought about saying, but you don't say too much to Uncle Guy. I could see why he was a policeman.

I called Kambui and said that we might get Sidney to see prison life and scare him away from drugs.

"You know what a guy told me?" Kambui asked. "He said it would be cheaper to give addicts free drugs than to put them in jail."

"It'd be cheaper to shoot them, too," I said. "My uncle Guy said he'd see about showing Sidney something that would change his mind."

"Yeah, okay," Kambui said. "Look, what did you do today?"

"Went down and watched my mother shoot a commercial," I said. "She did it in English and then they dubbed in some Japanese over her so it looked as if she was speaking Japanese."

"You ever wonder why people speak different languages?" Kambui asked. "I can see it in the old days when everybody was separate, but now that what happens gets around the world in two seconds I don't see why we don't just settle on one language so we could understand each other."

"And we wouldn't have to take language in school."

"And you know what else I was thinking?" Kambui went on. "In Africa they have languages with different kinds of sounds, not just regular syllables. Swahili has clicks in it. How do you teach kids how to do that?"

Good point.

THE CRUISER

A TRIP TO THE LIBRARY

By Zander Scott

What I wondered was why didn't we have clicks and whistles and maybe even a few hums in English. So I took a trip to the library. The old subway car rumbled and rattled all the way downtown before coming to a screeching halt at 42nd Street. I ran up the stairs, huffing and puffing all the way, because I knew it was late. Phew, just made it before closing time! I shuffled up to the third-floor reading room. The librarian put her fingers to her lips and shushed me. I didn't know what was bugging her because I had squelched all the noises except the rustle of paper as I got ready to take notes.

"How come we don't have any hums and clicks in English?" I whispered.

Her eyes fluttered for a moment. "Huh?"

"I said, how come we don't have any hums and clicks in English?"

She pointed toward the computer and told me to Google the subject. I went over to the library PC and clicked on Internet Explorer. I could hear the hard drive whizzing for a moment and then stopping. I whacked the computer hard enough to hurt my hand.

"Ouch!"

"Shh!" A guy with horn-rimmed glasses.

The computer started up again, purring away, and then *poof!* a screen popped up saying that the library was now closed.

"Ugh!"

On the way back to the subway, I stopped at a small store, plunked my money down on the counter, and bought a soda. I snapped off the cap, watched it fizz for a minute, and then gurgled it down.

On the way uptown I realized I didn't care if English didn't have any clicks.

CHAPTER FIVE
Scared Straight, Kinda

The Cruisers are a very interesting group," Mrs. Maxwell said in the hallway. "You are very bright *and* very resourceful. I spoke to your uncle this morning."

"He was at the school?"

"No, he called for permission to take some of you on a field trip this Saturday afternoon," Mrs. Maxwell said. "I called the parents of all the Cruisers and they were quite concerned but understood what we are trying to do. Once they discovered that their own children were not involved with drugs they were quite cooperative. Oh, yes, and Cody Weinstein is going with you. Apparently, your uncle and his father played something together."

"Oh, good," I said. That sounded kind of lame but I was thinking as fast as I could. I didn't like Mr. Weinstein that much. He was a gym teacher and kind of jocky. He once told me that I could play better basketball if I got a lot tougher. I thought he meant to play nastier, and I didn't like that. His son, Cody, was the best athlete in the school and could play any sport, but he wasn't on any team his father coached, which was football and soccer. He played basketball well and was always up-front with what he said. I liked him a lot. I was even thinking of asking him to join the Cruisers.

When Mrs. Maxwell said we were going on a field trip in the afternoon I thought she meant right after lunch. It turned out she meant after school.

We had agreed to meet on Morningside Avenue and 125th Street, in front of St. Joseph's. Kambui and I got there first and then Bobbi and then LaShonda.

"Suppose Sidney doesn't show up?" Bobbi asked.

"Cody is going to pick him up," I said. "He said if there was a problem he'd call me."

"Suppose a prisoner grabs us . . . or something," Bobbi said. "Some of these guys have been locked up for years."

"Then I'll turn Zander loose on them," Kambui said. "He'll bust out with his Tae Kwon Do and it'll be all over. They'll be in lockdown and Zander will be writing it up for *The Cruiser*. Ain't that right, Zander?"

"It's the word you heard," I said.

Cody and Sidney showed up in a gypsy cab a minute later. Cody had on jeans and a polo shirt, looking like an advertisement from JCPenney, and Sidney had on a suit and a bow tie.

"Don't crack on the bow tie," LaShonda whispered as we watched them get out of the cab.

We all gave Sidney and Cody high fives and tried to make small talk but I dug that Sidney's eyes were already getting bigger. He was scared before the scaring got started.

Uncle Guy showed up with a van marked NEW YORK POLICE DEPARTMENT, and Cody and the Cruisers piled in, with Kambui and Bobbi leading the way.

"Did you see some of the vendors looking at us?" Kambui asked. "They were probably wondering what we were doing going with the police."

"They're probably going to think we're undercover cops," Cody said.

"We got black guys with us," Bobbi said. "They'll probably think we're felons."

I had called Sidney and told him that I wanted to show him something and that maybe that would help him make up his mind about messing with drugs.

"I don't think I can be helped," he'd answered.

He sounded real bad on the phone and I wondered if he was more into drugs than we knew about. I remembered what he had said once about playing chess, that in any position there were good moves and then there was the best move.

"Sometimes, when things look terrible," he had said, "you just need to find the right move to turn the whole game around. When you find it you feel great."

I wondered why he wasn't looking for the right move to get himself away from being a drug addict.

Uncle Guy was in the front of the van with another man he introduced as Officer Riley. Riley was my height, had a flat nose and a wide jaw that seemed to go right down into his neck. He looked like he could have beat up a truck. Uncle Guy said Riley worked with him in investigating drug cases. When he said that, Sidney looked away.

We drove uptown to 145th Street and across the bridge. That was weird because I thought we were going to be driving across town to the Triborough Bridge and over to Rikers Island. Rikers is the biggest prison complex in the country.

"The Bronx," Cody said, "home of the New York Yankees."

We drove down some small streets and nobody in the van had anything to say. We stopped in front of a building off Morris Park Avenue.

"We're here," Uncle Guy said. "And from now on I don't want anybody making any wisecracks, no jokes, no loud talking. Anybody here don't understand that?"

Nobody spoke. I could feel my heart beating hard in my chest and the palms of my hands were sweating. I looked at the building. It looked deserted. Some of the windows were boarded up. There was what looked like a plastic tricycle on the fire escape above us. A torn blind flapped from a window on the top floor. But there was music coming from one of the apartments so I knew that someone must live there. I realized I was holding my breath.

There was a police officer on the top step.

"All clear," he said to Uncle Guy.

"Okay, stay together," Uncle Guy said. "We're only going to be here a minute or so."

We all got out and Officer Riley locked the van, which was kind of funny because it said NEW YORK CITY POLICE right on the side and I didn't think anybody would break into it. Then Uncle Guy led us into the building.

The place was dark and dingy and the stench of urine was strong enough to make me want to throw up. Bobbi reached over and took my hand. Uncle Guy walked up the stairs slowly and I could feel my heart beating even faster as the stairs creaked beneath my feet. Kambui, LaShonda, and Cody went right behind him, with me, Bobbi, and Sidney after them. Riley followed us and I knew they were protecting us.

We heard a noise and Bobbi jumped. A tall, thin man with a tattoo on his face came down the stairs. He had a pit bull on a leash and when he saw us he pulled the dog close to his leg.

"Move against the wall," Uncle Guy said to the man, and he did.

I didn't want to look at the dude as we passed and I don't think anybody else did, either.

We stopped on the second floor in front of a door at the end of the hallway and Uncle Guy motioned for us to move in close. The hall was dimly lit and spooky. Bobbi, who was usually smiling, looked grim as she moved against me.

"Okay, as I said, we're only going to be here a minute and then we're going to move on," Uncle Guy said.

I looked at Officer Riley. He was looking serious.

Uncle Guy pushed the door open and stepped inside. A moment later a light came on and we saw it was a small bathroom.

"Look around," Office Riley said.

It was funny, but we were just about too scared to look inside. None of us wanted to step into the bathroom, but after a while we all did.

The room was small, with a bathtub against the far wall. There was a toilet that had some kind of dark stuff in it that I didn't want to think about, and a small sink that was mostly yellow and chipped. The smell was kind of bad and it was dirty, especially the bathtub. There were crumpled advertising brochures in the tub and a torn, dirty cigarette pack lying on the greenish stain that led to the drain.

"Before this building was upgraded they used to have one bathroom per floor," Uncle Guy said. "It's a lot better now, with most of the apartments having their own bathrooms. Okay, we ready to leave?"

We were and Riley led us back downstairs and out onto the street. There were people on the street who looked at us as we got into the van. They looked like poor people.

Down-and-outs. When Riley was back in the driver's seat, Uncle Guy handed us an envelope.

"Take the pictures out," he said.

We took out three pictures. They were of a girl who looked twelve, maybe even younger. She was white, kind of cute, with dark brown hair and a pretty smile. The pictures were of her near a Christmas tree. The house she was in looked nice. One of the pictures showed one end of a piano. There were porcelain elephants lined up on it.

We passed the pictures around and then gave them back to Uncle Guy when he reached for them.

"These are the pictures her family gave us when we were looking for her," he said. "That bathroom is where we found her body."

It was, like — whoa! My whole body felt numb and none of us said anything as the van moved away from the curb.

Uncle Guy and Riley started talking as we pulled off. Riley said the pictures were copies, not the originals. Uncle Guy looked at them again. He was talking about what they could do with digital pictures.

We went to one more place. It was a vacant lot near 181st Street across from a used furniture store. Uncle Guy had us walk to a corner of the lot. There were broken bottles, tin cans, a picture frame with images of an angel watching two kids cross a bridge, a woolen sweater, and newspapers strewn around. I found myself looking for signs a body had been there, but I didn't see any.

When we got back to the van Uncle Guy showed us another picture. It was a teenage black guy. He looked a little like Kambui. There was a clipping with the picture about how he had scored twenty-two points in a basketball game.

"He was a nice kid," Uncle Guy said. "He had a scholarship offer to go to North Carolina A&T. His parents are nice people, too. The father worked — where'd he work, Riley?"

"Was that the big guy who worked at Bellevue?"

"Yeah, that was him," Uncle Guy said. "Never understood how his kid could mess with drugs. Just never understood how a good kid with that much potential . . ."

"It's always like that," Riley said. "You trace the DOAs back and you find a sweet kid somewhere along the line. It's always like that."

I knew that DOA meant dead on arrival. I felt a little like crying.

Uncle Guy took us back to 125th Street.

"You guys can keep the pictures if you want," Riley said. "We have the parents' permission."

We didn't want them.

"There's professional help available if anybody has a drug problem," he said. "We know that it's a medical problem and there are people who can deal with it. On the other hand, I have more pictures if anybody needs to see them."

We all hugged each other before we split up. Bobbi was the most shook up and I asked her if she wanted me to take her home.

"No," she said. "I'm good. Just got some thinking to do."

Sidney thanked me and said that my uncle was pretty cool. We were standing in front of the train station on St. Nicholas Avenue.

"I think I need to do a lot of thinking, too," he said. "Maybe I should just drop out for a while and get my head together."

"My uncle said that there's medical help available," I said. "You want me to talk to Mr. Culpepper?"

"I think he hates me," Sidney said. "You ever see the way he looks at me?"

"He doesn't hate you," I said. "He really wants you on the chess team."

"I think he hates me," Sidney said as he turned toward the subway stairs. "I gotta go."

THE CRUISER

I'M SORRY . . . A LIST POEM

By Bobbi McCall

I'm sorry for the kids in magazines

Their sad faces peering from terrible scenes

I'm sorry for the kids who can't be found

Or beg for food and sleep on the ground

I'm sorry for kids with parents in tears

Because some driver needed a few more beers

I'm sorry for kids in documentaries

Or kids looking miserable in cemeteries

I'm sorry for the kids who have been abused

And whose whole lives have been misused

I'm sorry for kids whose hearts are pure

But are dying of diseases that we can cure

I'm sorry for these kids but I also feel shame

For being glad these lists don't include my name

CHAPTER SIX
LaShonda, LaWonda, La Shakespeare . . . Who Knew?

I have decided that I do not like white people!" LaShonda was shouting into the phone again.

"Yo, baby, what's wrong?" I asked.

"Zander, I am *not* your baby and I am *not* your mama so don't go calling me out my name," LaShonda said at the same earsplitting decibel level.

"Okay, so what is happening, Miss LaShonda Powell?"

"They are up-and-downing me," she said. "This morning the weatherman tells me that it's going to be nice out. Then when I get to school I see it's starting to rain."

"And he was white?"

"No, he was black, but that don't matter."

"Okay."

"Then Miss Ortiz looks me right in the face and tells

me that I don't get extra credit for turning my essay in on time even though I was one of the *only* ones — can you spell *only?* — who turned theirs in on time."

"That's not a downer," I said.

"It is when you got a C on it and was hoping for some extra credit to push you up to a B," she said.

"Okay."

"Okay? Okay?" LaShonda's voice went up in pitch. "Then the bad stuff started happening. I got to the house and there was a letter waiting for me — which is good news because I don't get much mail — and it's from *LaFemme.* I think it's just a letter saying my poem has been rejected as usual but they're talking about publishing my poem."

"In *LaFemme?*" I asked. "That's great news. That's, like, really big-time. *LaFemme* is the biggest new magazine out there. They're actually going to publish you?"

"If I cut down on the lines of my beautiful poem!" LaShonda said. "They're talking about me reading something on Shakespeare and his sonnets. Man, this was a poem I wrote when I came back from that bathroom where that girl died. I can't just cut stuff like that."

"You going to tell them no?"

"How am I going to do that when they're offering me a hundred dollars and saying they're going to publish me in *LaFemme*?" LaShonda said.

"You got to do something," I said.

"Well, what I'm working on is hating white people," LaShonda said. "They're probably white over at that magazine, right?"

"I don't know," I said. "But you must have wanted to write for it or you wouldn't have sent it over to them."

"True, but that doesn't change anything," LaShonda said. "And I knew you wouldn't understand because you're a guy."

"Why don't you just look on the positive side of things?" I said. "If you get published in *LaFemme*, everybody has to give you your propers. Plus you cop a Benjamin. It all sounds good to me."

"That's what I was thinking," LaShonda said. "When another white dude shows up in my American dream. Sidney got busted again."

"Get out of here!"

"If I'm lying, I'm flying!" LaShonda said. "Bigmouth Phat Tony called Kambui and told him that this chick he was going out with from the DR — and I don't believe it because he's too ugly to have a girlfriend — told him that a guy from our school got picked up trying to buy drugs on Avenue B and everybody thought he was an undercover cop because he looked so white and a real undercover cop busted him."

"So how you know it's Sidney?"

"Phat Tony said she described him. He was white and he said he went to Da Vinci."

Okay, so it sounded like Sidney. I told LaShonda I would check it out and she asked me if I would help her cut her poem down.

"I thought you said you weren't going to cut it down," I said.

"If I sell out will you still like me?" she asked.

What was I suppose to say behind that?

"Yeah," I said.

Okay, so I was getting uptight about the whole Sidney thing. The Cruisers were sending out a lifeline and my man was steadily cutting it into pieces. What was up with that?

We had talked to Sidney and the conversation hadn't really gone anywhere. We had gotten my uncle Guy to show us some scary-ass things and they had scared me half to death and everybody, but Sidney was still going strong on the drug scene. I was thinking about him maybe sitting in a jail cell looking through the bars, or maybe some big guys looking to beat him up or even have sex with him. I had seen some hard things on television.

What I knew was that I was lost. I didn't know what to think.

Mom came home. She was all made-up in her I'm-not-wearing-makeup outfit. She looked hot, which I didn't like because I didn't like thinking about my mom as looking hot even though it was her job.

"How you doing?" she asked, taking off the big floppy hat she was wearing.

"Not too good," I said. "I think my friend got busted for drugs again."

She stopped in the middle of the room, turned her head toward me, and sort of stretched out her neck like she was really peeping into me. "You want to talk to your father about this?"

"No."

"It might be best," she said.

"He know more about drugs than you do?"

"I doubt it," she said. "He knows more about coffee, though. What happened?"

"LaShonda said that Kambui said that this girl said that she heard that Sidney got busted."

"How many people did that message go through?" Mom asked. "Did you call his house?"

I shrugged and gave her a head shake. She picked up the phone and handed it to me.

I didn't really want to call Sidney because I didn't want to hear any more bad news about him. But then I was thinking about what Moms would do and I knew she might call my father. She was always afraid that she wouldn't do the right thing and that he would go to court and get an order or something saying I would have to go out to Seattle, Washington, and live with him and his new wife and their daughter. I was getting just about big enough to say I wouldn't do it and maybe run away but I knew it would mess with Mom if I ran away. I was getting to be sorry that I felt bad for Sidney. Which was lame. Which was big-time lame.

I dialed Sidney's number. If his grandfather answered the phone I thought I would speak in a West Indian accent and tell him that I was from the credit bureau and wanted to speak with Sidney. Then he would tell me if Sidney had been arrested. If his grandmother answered I would tell her that I was doing a survey of schoolkids around the country and wanted to speak to Sidney. She would like that.

"Hello?" His grandmother.

"Hello, I'm doing a survey of New York City students —"

"Hello, Alexander," his grandmother said. "How are you doing? Fine, I hope. I'll call Sidney."

Busted. I thought about hanging up, but I was glad that Sidney wasn't in jail.

"Hey!" Sidney.

"What happened, man?"

"I was really down, Zander," Sidney said. "I had to get some chill pills."

Chill pills? Sidney was slipping into the vocabulary too easily. It was like he was on the scene and *playing* the scene at the same time. I don't know why I thought there was more to the Sidney story than he was telling, but I did. It was just a feeling. But it was a strong feeling.

○○○○○○○○○○○○○○○○○○○○○○○○○○○○○○○○○○○○○○

Okay, so sometimes I'm just cool, and sometimes I feel really talented, and sometimes I feel gifted in a roundabout kind of way, and sometimes I'm simply awesome. I was lying in bed thinking about Sidney when I also started thinking about this poet Miss Ortiz told us about named François Villon. Villon was a poet but he was also a crook and a street dude. He was in jail for years and also was condemned to death a couple of times. He was smart, and he was a writer. The writing changed his life, made him a respected dude in French literature instead of just a murderer and a jailbird. Oscar Wilde had also been in jail, and Malcolm X. I was thinking that if I got Sidney to write about his problem it could put a new perspective on it. I called Bobbi.

"So you're going to get Sidney to write about using drugs?" she asked. "That's, like, a confession. They could put him in jail and then it would be your fault."

"No, he can write about anything he wants," I said. "Remember when Miss Ortiz was talking about how some famous writers worked out their problems by writing stories?"

"Go on."

"Well, maybe if Sidney wrote about his problems he

would work them out by himself," I said. "And if it was anything incriminating, we wouldn't publish it."

"Just tell him to write anything he wants?"

"That way there's no pressure," I said.

"Call me back and let me know if he's going to do it," Bobbi said.

I didn't want to call her back, I wanted her to do it. I said okay, though, and then I called Kambui.

"Yo, Kambui, I was thinking about Sidney," I said. "This thing is really getting to me."

"What are you doing?"

"Trying to figure out Sidney's problem," I said.

"No, I mean right now. You sitting at the table? You eating a sandwich? What are you doing?"

"I'm lying on the floor right next to my dumbbells thinking maybe I'll get to some exercise," I said. "What you doing?"

"I'm texting Zhade Hopkins," Kambui said. "I'm thinking about asking her to go out with me."

"Zhade is too fine for you," I said.

"No, I think she digs me," Kambui said. "I think you and I should go out with her and her sister. On a double date."

"Where do you want to take them?"

"Never mind, she just texted me back and called me a frog," Kambui said. "Why did she have to go there?"

"Maybe she's hoping to kiss you and turn you into a handsome prince," I said.

"I didn't like her anyway."

Lie.

"So, getting back to Sidney," I went on. "I think he knows drugs are bad but he hasn't really seen how bad so he's, like, into some kind of movie version."

"What movie?"

"I don't know, man, *some* movie," I said. "It's, like, you see guys get shot in pictures and then the next day you see them on television talking about how good the film was. It makes the killing part not too bad."

"So you think we should get him some heavy drugs and let him OD or something?" Kambui asked.

"This afternoon I told him that we wanted to publish a picture of a crackhead in *The Cruiser*," I said. "I asked him if he could get us one."

"Look, Zander, I know you and Sidney are friends," Kambui said. "But as far as I'm concerned he's just weirding out. Maybe all that chess he plays has got his head twisted. You know — mad genius stuff?"

"The guy's a chess wizard," I said. "Plus, he's a good guy and he goes to our school. I was shocked when he got arrested for trying to buy drugs. If he does come up with a picture I'm going to put it in *The Cruiser*."

"I don't see how it's going to help," Kambui said. "But it doesn't cost anything, so why not?"

"I have to do *something*," I said.

"I got to get to my homework," Kambui said. "I have fifteen thousand more pages to read."

"You think if I texted Zhade and asked her about us double-dating with her and her sister she might say yes?" I asked.

"I wouldn't even go out with her now," Kambui said. "Where did she get that frog bit?"

"That was kind of cold," I said.

Kambui said he had to finish his homework and would see me in school. When I had hung up it was easy to see that Kambui was more into Zhade than he was into Sidney's problems. But Kambui was my main man and I knew he would be thinking about it. That's the way he is. You say something to him and you think he's forgotten about it

and then two or three weeks later — *bam!* — he's right back on the case.

I was still lying on the floor when Mom came to the door and pointed to the cell phone she was holding. Somebody was calling for me and she wanted to know if I wanted to answer it. She put the phone behind her back and said it was a lady.

For a wild moment I thought it was going to be Zhade. Zhade is so hot she can melt a Hershey bar from across the room just by looking at it. It wasn't Zhade, it was Bobbi calling me back.

"Hey, Zander, I've got the game with Powell all figured out." She was chirping again. She does that when she's happy. "I have four numbers. If we manage to get three of them we'll win."

"The first number is one," I said. "If we get one more point than the other team, we'll win."

"The first number is nine," Bobbi continued, ignoring me. "One player has to get nine rebounds. The second number —"

"Why nine?" I asked.

"The second number is seventy. That has to be our free-throw percentage."

"Where are you getting these numbers?"

"Each number represents a phase of the game that we have to dominate," she said.

"You're not playing, Bobbi," I said. "We're playing."

"I'm giving you the tools to win the game," Bobbi said. "So it's nine rebounds by one player, seventy percent of our free throws, the third is team assists — we need nine — and the last number is thirty-five. We need to hit thirty-five percent of our three-point tries. That's it. What do you think?"

"Bobbi, you don't know diddly-squat about basketball," I said.

"Yeah, I do," Bobbi said. "Because it's really about numbers and percentages."

"So what do you think about Sidney's problem?"

"What do you think about my math solution?"

"We'll check it out when we play Powell on Thursday," I said. "And if we get those numbers and lose we'll burn you at the stake."

"And if you win you can put a photo of me in the trophy case," Bobbi said.

"Can we get back to Sidney?" I asked.

"He's the best player on our team," Bobbi said. "I'm second board, John Brendel is third, and Todd Balf is fourth."

"I could probably beat all of you with my eyes closed," I said.

"In your dreams, baby," Bobbi said. "In your dreams!"

Okay, the basketball team, Bobbi, LaShonda, Kambui, and Ashley Schmidt from the school newspaper, *The Palette*, went all the way to 147th Street and Amsterdam Avenue to play against Adam Clayton Powell. On the way Bobbi kept passing around her numbers.

"Zander, you have to get the nine rebounds," she said. "You're the tallest."

"The secret to basketball," Coach Law said, "is having the will to win. Without that will you're going to lose."

"Numbers don't lie," Bobbi said. "Numbers are a way that God slips us the truth."

"Spoken like a true young lady," Coach Law said.

"Spoken like a sexist basketball coach," LaShonda said.

Coach Law grinned.

Powell's basketball team was okay but I didn't like them because the whole school thought they were hot stuff.

They had had Mae Jemison come up to the school once, and President Clinton and some author from New Jersey, so they thought they were special.

"Can you get nine boards?" Cody asked me.

"Yeah."

"If you keep crashing the boards you'll get fouled," Cody said. "I'll drive more down the lane so I should pick up a couple of fouls, and the whole team will work on assists."

Coach Law kept talking about the will to win and Cody kept looking at Bobbi's numbers. I was wondering if Cody was going soft on Bobbi. Ashley had a copy of Bobbi's numbers, too, and she wanted to write them up in *The Palette*.

The game started and I gave up everything to work on the boards. The dude I was up against, a West Indian brother I knew, was strong and did a lot of pushing but he couldn't really sky. I was snatching bounds pretty easy.

The whole thing was that all of us went into the game with Bobbi's numbers in our heads. It was a little freaky at first, but I didn't want to fall down on my count.

In the end we beat them. No, we crushed them. Okay, we left them bleeding and whimpering on the court! Cody scored thirty points and was getting so mean I had to help

Powell defend him. I only scored sixteen points because I'm a merciful kind of guy.

I felt great about the game and especially about beating Powell. But the way that Ashley wrote it up in *The Palette* you would have thought that Bobbi beat Powell all by herself.

I saw Kambui in the media center and he asked me if Bobbi was going to replace me on the team.

"I just hope the coach doesn't fall in love with those numbers," I said.

"Did Sidney show up with a picture of a crackhead?"

"No, he gave me a picture of a chessboard with numbers on it," I said. "Very strange. But we'll publish it just to make him feel good."

Kambui said that publishing something that didn't make sense was stupid. I wanted to help Sidney but I didn't want to do stupid stuff. I had given the chessboard to Bobbi to put together with the stuff we were going to publish in the next issue of *The Cruiser*. Now I wasn't sure and texted her saying that maybe we shouldn't publish it.

if it don't mean anything lets not do it Z-Man

Z-Man, wake ↑ it's a simple substitution code figure it out -- Bad-B

01010	01111	10010	11100	00110	00010	01001	00110
11000	11000	01010	01001	00000	11001	00110	00001
00110	01010	10001	01000	00000	11000	11001	00000
10111	11001	01001	00110	10100	10111	00110	11000
11000	11010	10111	00110	01010	11000	11001	00110
10111	10111	01010	00001	01111	00110	10100	01111
00110	00000	11000	00110	01001	00110	01111	10100
10000	00110	11000	01010	00100	10001	00110	11111

SHADOWS

By LaShonda Powell (sent to LaFemme)

There are scary things

That lurk in the corners

That bump and creak in the shadows

There are clouds that chill

The damp hallways

Filling the cracks beneath the doors

Muffling the sadness

Stifling the sobs

An odor like flowers at a funeral

Floats inches above the floor

Sweet fragrance of death

Sticking to the skin

Mixing with the sweat of fear

They say that smell

Is close to taste

It is bitter, and I must swallow

Eyes closed, arms folded

Kids I never knew

Lie curled in tight circles

Dreaming of better times

There is a small square room

In the corner of my heart

It lies behind a door

I hope I never open

CHAPTER SEVEN
The Da Vinci Code

"A nother teenager got shot in the Bronx," Mom said. "A young girl. And you know the sad part about it?"

"She got killed?"

"No, but she's fighting for her life," Mom said. "The sad part about it is that it didn't even make the front page. Don't you think that's sad?"

"Yeah." I knew what she meant, that a girl got shot and it wasn't a big thing. I looked over Mom's shoulder and moved her hand so that I could see what had made the front page. It was a story about a girl rapper throwing her shoe at a cop. There was a picture of the girl and she looked really mad. I had heard some of her raps and they weren't anything special. "I guess people being shot isn't a big deal."

"She's Puerto Rican," Mom said.

"You think that makes a difference?"

"My grandfather used to say that, when he was a boy, if a black person got shot or killed you had to wait until Thursday to find the details," Mom said. "That's when the black newspaper came out. They didn't print news about black people in the white papers."

"Really?"

"Really," Mom said. "You can tell a lot about how well people are doing just from what's written about them in the newspapers."

That gave me a whole idea in one sentence. Bobbi was going to deal with basketball and numbers and I liked that, but maybe we could also check out how different kinds of people were being treated by just looking at old newspapers and seeing how they were covered. I told the idea to Mom and she didn't like it.

"You'd have to read five hundred thousand newspapers," she said. "What are you giving up? Basketball? Sleep?"

I still thought it was a good idea.

At first everyone was saying that the chessboard and numbers that Sidney published in *The Cruiser* represented a perfect chess game. Then they were saying that the numbers were New York City zip codes. That made more sense.

"It's got nothing to do with zip codes," Bobbi said. "It's a simple substitution code."

"You know what it says?" Kambui asked.

"Yes, but I think maybe we should let Sidney tell us." Bobbi was painting her fingernails black. "The message is kind of personal."

"If we're going to be the ones who help him, we need to know what the problem is," Kambui said.

"If we're going to be the ones who help him then we'd better make sure that we *can* help him," Bobbi said, looking up from across the lunchroom table. "And we need to know if he *wants* our help."

"So what you saying we should do?" Kambui asked.

"Sidney and I are going to a chess tournament Saturday to watch Jamie Pullman, a student at Thurgood Marshall Academy," Bobbi said. "He's first board. Why don't you guys come and we can talk to Sidney casually after the match."

"I can't go," Kambui said. "I'm working Saturday."

I said I could go and Bobbi and I agreed to meet at her house in Brooklyn. The chess tournament was being held at the Brooklyn Public Library, which was only a few blocks from where she lived.

"I don't get all the mystery," Kambui said. "Why can't you just tell us what the message is and get it over with?"

"You don't understand why Sidney is messing with drugs, either," Bobbi answered. "But he's got a real problem and your simple answers don't always work."

"Yo, dig Bobbi." Kambui pointed his index finger across the table at Bobbi. "She just joined a new terrorist group — Al Calculus."

"You're mixing two language groups, Arabic and Latin," Bobbi said. "The *Al* is from the Arabic, and *Calculus* has a Latin root."

"Shut up," Kambui replied.

I could see that Kambui was getting mad so I said I had to go to the media center. He told Bobbi that her nails looked stupid and that the Cruisers weren't about going goth. Bobbi said that as far as she was concerned the Cruisers might not be about anything soon. She said that to Kambui but she was looking dead at me.

I remembered what she had told me about Mr. Culpepper still wanting to break up the Cruisers, when I saw Caren Culpepper in the hall and caught up with her.

"Hey, Caren, what's happening?"

"Nothing."

"Hey, I heard your father was trying to bring some grief to the Cruisers," I said.

"You think he's racist?"

"Racist?" I looked at Caren to see if she was serious. She was. "What makes you think that?"

She shrugged and turned into one of the classrooms. I followed her into her Geography classroom. When she started taking some books off the shelf I put my hand on them to stop her.

"He said something?"

"Zander, you're black and I'm white. So why don't you call my father and tell him you would like to take me out Friday night," Caren said, looking over her glasses. "See what he says."

I felt my stomach jump, as if I was afraid. Caren didn't look at me, just took the books and went to her desk.

Race wasn't something I was comfortable dealing with. Even if I felt someone was wrong I wasn't easy talking about it or confronting them.

The thing was that I always felt bad talking about race but I always thought I should do something if people were coming down hard on black people. Mr. Culpepper hadn't said anything against blacks — I didn't think he liked anybody — but I thought that maybe Caren had heard him say something.

Marc, Mom's agent, came over for dinner. He brought a huge bag of hamburgers, sodas, and French fries. He was all excited, talking about a perfume gig for Mom.

"Perfume is the gateway to high fashion," he said, wiping some mustard from his chin. "And high fashion is where the money is."

"What do I have to do?" Mom asked.

"The way the director laid it out to me is this." Marc put his burger down and held his hands up with the palms out. "You're in a dark room. They can barely see you. Behind you, in the distance, there's New York at midnight. Maybe a few cars pass. Then there's a small light on you and we see your profile. Then a male voice asks, 'New perfume?' Then you hesitate for a beat and say, 'If you think so.' That's it!"

"If I'm in the shadows and they don't see me, how's that helping my career?"

"It's building you up as a woman of mystery," Marc said.

Mom rolled her eyes toward the ceiling. "Will they see the guy?"

"Only his hand holding a glass of champagne," Marc said. "It's going to be interracial, too."

"Is that good?"

"It can't hurt," Marc said.

I thought about what Caren had said. I got a burger, a handful of fries, and started toward my room.

"What do you think, Zander man?" Marc called to me.

"Sounds okay, I guess," I said.

Everyone in the school had two numbers they had to carry with them all the time. One was Mrs. Maxwell's and the other was Mr. Culpepper's. I called our assistant principal, waited for four rings, and was just about ready to hang up when he answered.

"Hello, Mr. Culpepper, this is Alexander Scott," I said.

"And?"

"Uh, I wonder if I could take Caren to the movies this Friday," I managed to get out without hiccuping.

"One moment. *Caren!*" I heard Caren answer in the background. "Do you want to go to a movie with Alexander Scott this Friday?"

She said yes.

"Alexander?"

"Yes, sir?"

"I will expect you between six-thirty and seven, and I will expect you to bring my daughter safely home by ten-thirty, is that understood?"

"Yes, sir."

The phone clicked.

I hung up.

Back into the living room. Marc is showing Mom a bottle of perfume. It looks fancy.

"Zander, are you okay?" Mom pushes the perfume away.

"I just got a date with Caren Culpepper," I said.

"I don't know her, do I?" Mom said. "Is that wonderful?"

THE PALETTE

Question: Should Da Vinci lose its elite status and be open to all students whether they are classified as gifted and talented or not? These essays were written after a discussion moderated by Ashley Schmidt and Mr. Finley.

No!

By Kelly Bena, eighth grade

Gifted and Talented is, perhaps, a bad name for our school. It would be fairer to call the school Hard Work Academy. We are in Da Vinci because we do the work necessary to do well. If we have special status it is because we maintain high enough standards to deserve that status. Bringing in students who are not willing to do the work is no favor to them and lessens the opportunities of those currently working our butts off to make Da Vinci a great place in which to learn.

Yes!

By Demetrius Brown, seventh grade

Maybe everybody would do the work if they felt special. When you play guitar it's the top four strings that usually play the melody and everybody is happy with them, but the bottom two strings are valuable also and provide the harmonics. Having a school like Da Vinci is like having a school for the top strings when, eventually, all of the strings are needed to make beautiful music. Also, there is a lot of pressure to show that you are gifted when sometimes you only want to be yourself.

No!

By Alvin McCraney, eighth grade

The reason we have elite schools is that we have elite gene pools. Some people are just smarter than others and we have to face that fact. Why hold the smart kids back just so we can get along with the not-so-smarts? People who know things, who really know things, understand that it's going to be the smart people who will be the leaders of tomorrow and who will do the inventing, write the books, and create the government that will be of most benefit to all people (including the not-so-smarts!).

Yes!

By Bobbi McCall, eighth grade

The reason we should not have elite schools is that jean pools can be created by anyone.

If I want my jeans shrunk so that they will fit me perfectly I can put them in a big pool created by someone with an IQ of 200 or an IQ of 55. As a matter of fact I left one pair of jeans out on my fire escape by accident and it rained on them and shrank them down. And as far as the leaders of tomorrow . . . have you ever heard of a war being started by anyone wearing tight jeans? No, you have not. It's the baggy pants people of the world who start wars! 'Nuff said?

Editor's note: I am sorry that the representative from The Cruiser *did not take this subject seriously, as we think she could have made a real contribution.*

CHAPTER EIGHT
Papa Was a Strolling Pawn

I met Bobbi at the coffee shop on the first floor of the Brooklyn Public Library. She pointed to an empty table and I grabbed it while she went for sodas. A geeky-looking guy came over and asked if the other two chairs at the table were taken.

"One of them is," I said.

"Which one?" he asked.

"The one my friend is going to sit in," I said, pulling his chain.

He looked at both of the chairs, then at me, and then walked away.

Bobbi came back and plopped down. "I forgot to ask you what kind of soda you want," she said, "so I got an orange soda for me and cola for you."

"I don't like cola," I said.

"Then I spit in the orange soda so I would be sure to get it," she said, not missing a beat.

I took the cola.

We waited fifteen minutes for Sidney. For some reason I thought he would show up half drugged and maybe smoking a joint or something. He didn't. We knew he had arrived when the sound level went up about a half twist. A couple of the kids started taking pictures. I turned to see who they were taking pictures of and saw Sidney. He had shown up wearing a suit, a tie, and sunglasses.

"Yo, they're treating him like he's a star," I said.

"In this crowd he is," Bobbi said, waving past me to some Asian kids sitting across the floor. "These are all chess players from across the country. They're here to see Pullman play."

"He really that good?"

"Jamie Pullman played the King's Gambit against a master last week and cooked him," Bobbi said. Sidney was just reaching our table. "Pullman goes eighteen hundred to two thousand all year and then busts a master with a King's Gambit? That's like you going up against LeBron James one-on-one and shutting him out."

"How you guys doing?" This from Sidney.

"I'm good," Bobbi said.

"I'm Zander," I said. "You can draw your conclusions from that. How you doing?"

"Pullman is playing Sam Manzi," Sidney said. "No big deal. He's a world-class hockey player but just a bit above average in chess. You just sit long enough and Manzi gets impatient and starts hurrying up his moves. He's a fast-twitch dude in a slow-twitch game."

"Yeah, but if you fall behind Manzi you won't make it up," Bobbi said. "But I still don't know how Pullman got by with the King's Gambit against a master unless the guy was having a bad day."

"You ever play Pullman?" I asked Sidney.

"Two draws," Sidney said. "He played Sicilians both times. I think he's going to try the King's Gambit against me."

"*And?*"

"The next time they play, Sidney will be Black, so Pullman starts the game," Bobbi said. "He's got all of the book openings down pat and relies on a strong middle game. You make a mistake and it's death. It's going to be a fun match."

They were talking like gunslingers. I liked it even though I didn't know what they were talking about half the time.

We were sitting having drinks like we were in Dodge City waiting for the big shoot-out at the O.K. Corral.

Bobbi was doing more talking than Sidney, and I sensed that my man was getting freaked out by the pressure.

A short black guy came to the drinks area, stood between the tables, and then did a little flip-doodle move with his hand for us to get up. All of the geeks and geekettes got up and started toward the stairs.

Okay, so this is how the match was set up. There was a small stage and four chessboards on four tables. Each table had a clock and a chessboard. Above the tables were four computer screens, each with a chessboard and the names of the players. On board number one Pullman was playing a girl named Bashir.

"She any good?"

"She has a 1850 rating in Kenya," Bobbi whispered to me. "But you can't trust a foreign rating. I think she's a rainbow trout."

"Which means *what*?"

"Cute, but still a fish."

"Is she a nun?"

"No, Zander, she's Muslim," Bobbi said. "That's the *niqab*, the veil that some Muslim women wear."

Very cool.

The games moved along slowly, with the geeks and geekettes watching them, analyzing every move and playing them on their own chessboards or on their laptops. For me, it was boring.

"What do you think?" Bobbi leaned over and whispered to Sidney.

"She's going to force a draw against him if he isn't careful," Sidney said.

"You talking about Bashir against Pullman?" I asked.

"It's the only game anybody is watching," Bobbi said.

I couldn't tell who was winning and I was ready to leave. Nobody was making any noise, they weren't selling hot dogs, they didn't have any foxy cheerleaders, but they were *intense*!

Bobbi seemed cool, but she was playing the game on her laptop. Every time either Pullman or Bashir made a move she would make the same move and then she and Sidney would look it over. Bobbi kept looking at Sidney when Pullman made a move. Sometimes he would nod, at other times he would give a little shrug.

"How's he doing?" I asked.

"Okay, but I think he expected to have her by this time,"

Sidney said. He was leaning forward, sitting on the edge of the chair. "He hasn't broken out of any of the usual variations so far. She could be playing from memory. He's got to break that."

"Memory of what?"

A bunch of heads turned toward me when I raised my voice. I leaned forward and asked Sidney again, "Memory of *what*?"

"Most players have the openings memorized through the first twenty or so moves," he said. "Even the variations. But he's tippy-toeing around waiting for her to make a mistake. She's tippy-toeing around waiting for him to make a mistake. It's going to look bad if he doesn't get a full point against her."

I knew that a full point meant a win and a half point meant a draw.

"He should take her inside and slam-dunk over her," I said, smiling.

Sidney didn't smile. Neither did Bobbi.

I sat. I watched the game. I sat some more.

Then Sidney slapped my arm. "He made his move!" he said.

"He got her?"

"No, it's a trap," Sidney said. "But it's risky."

Around the room I saw the other kids who were watching move around in their seats. They all knew something was up. I looked at the screen. I didn't see anything.

"Bobbi," I whispered, "I don't see anything."

"He's going after her knight," Bobbi whispered.

I didn't see it. I looked at her knight and it looked fine to me.

We waited, and waited, and waited, while Bashir considered her move.

The girl behind the veil rocked slowly forward and back. She seemed calm. I wondered if, behind the veil and the differences, she was nervous, if her heart was beating faster. Finally, after a long while, she reached out her incredibly skinny fingers and made a move.

There was a flurry of movement around the room as all of the spectators made the same move on their boards. Then, as if there was one simultaneous recognition of an event, there was a huge sigh that seemed to float to the ceiling.

Sidney slapped his hand against his forehead. Bobbi leaned back in her chair and seemed to slump downward.

"He lost his rook!" Sidney said. "It's over!"

There were a few more moves on the stage, quick moves that went on over the growing buzz from the onlookers. But it was clear that something important had happened and a few moments later I saw Pullman reach over and lay down his king. The game was over.

There was a brief smattering of applause. Bashir stood and put her head down.

"I would have kicked her butt," Bobbi said.

Some of the kids watching were already leaving, and when I saw Sidney and Bobbi standing I was ready to go, too. We went down the stairs to the first floor with Sidney reciting all of the mistakes he thought that Pullman had made.

"The biggest was playing the King's Gambit against a girl," Sidney said. "When he sent that pawn strolling out to the middle of the board she had to grab it, and you know she's going to have all the variations memorized. That's what girls do."

"Bull!" Bobbi said. "He thought he had an easy win and he played her easy. She just waited for him to blow and he blew! Case closed. Look, there's Pullman with his father. His father used to play at City University a thousand years ago."

I looked over at Pullman talking to a man only an inch

or so taller than he was. Mr. Pullman had shockingly white hair that stood out on all sides. He was looking at his son and kept pushing the chess player's head up so that he could look him in the eye.

"He's probably telling him the same thing you said," I began. I was going to say something about what Pullman would do if he played the Kenyan girl again, but then I saw it. Mr. Pullman slapped his son across the face.

It was shocking, almost as if I had been hit. The kid stepped back and looked around quickly, bringing his hand to his face and looking around the fingers. I knew how he felt. He was embarrassed for everyone to see his father hit him like that.

"What's that all about?" I asked.

"We're not supposed to lose," Sidney said softly.

I turned to Sidney and saw that his face was flushed. There were tears in his eyes. I could feel myself tearing up and I turned away from Sidney and Bobbi.

I hated to see kids get hit. Maybe even more than being hit myself. Pullman had made a mistake, had lost a chess game, but it wasn't all that bad.

Sidney had one hand on my sleeve and one behind Bobbi's back as we went toward the huge doors of the

Brooklyn Public Library. Outside there was a light rain that was moving people from the tables that fronted the library and off the stairs.

"I got to get home," Sidney was saying.

"You want to stop for a soda or something?" I asked, my voice cracking.

"I got to get home," he repeated.

"See you in school Monday," I called to Sidney as he started down the stairs.

"I never thought of chess as being that serious," I said.

"Look over there," Bobbi said, nodding toward our right.

I saw the Pullman kid and his father walking down the stairs. The kid was about three steps behind, head down. Some dudes who looked as if they might be from the islands were on the stairs, talking. They wore bright yellow-and-green jackets that were close enough in design for them to be in a club or something. On the plaza in front of the library the blue umbrellas looked like a modern painting over the white tables. There were colors everywhere. Only the Pullmans were in black and white.

"I love chess, but I hate being a star," Bobbi said. "That's what Sidney's message on the chessboard read in code. Now you know why."

THE CRUISER

THE TEN COMMANDMENTS

OF BEING A GOOD PARENT

By Kambui Owens

1. Thou shalt not hit thy child.

2. Thou shalt not be ashamed of thy child.

3. Thou shalt not wish thy child was more like another kid.

4. Thou shalt talk to thy child, not just yell.

5. Thou shalt not tell thy child how he should feel.

6. Thou shalt not tell thy child how he should think.

7. Thou shalt help thy child to feel good and think well.

8. Thou shalt be friendly to thy child.

9. Thou shalt not want thy child to be just like you.

10. Thou shalt love thy child.

CHAPTER NINE
The Plot Thickens

Zander, are you playing that child?" LaShonda asked me at lunch.

"Playing who?" I asked.

"Everybody's talking about you telling Caren you're in love with her," LaShonda said. "And I can't believe you fell in love that fast."

"What are you talking about?" I asked.

"What am I . . . ?" LaShonda's hand found her hip. "It's all over the school that you and Caren are going out this weekend and she's telling everybody about how you said you've been sweating her for over a year now and just got up the nerve to make your move! What you got in mind for that seventh-grader?"

"We're going out this weekend but . . . who told you I was in love with her?"

"Marie Castro told Evelyn Nesbitt who told Zhade and you know if you tell Zhade anything you might as well put it in the newspapers," LaShonda said.

"My grandmother said that she's seen guys get lynched for messing with young white girls," Kambui added.

"I didn't know this train went to Stupid City," I said. "I'm not *messing* with Caren, I'm just taking her to the movies."

"I don't like that girl all that much, but don't use her, Zander," LaShonda said.

I watched as LaShonda slung her book bag over one shoulder and stalked off.

Kambui shook his head and left our table right after LaShonda.

"Yo, Bobbi, you know anything about this?" I asked.

"I think sometimes Caren makes up stuff," Bobbi said. "When we were in elementary school she told everybody her house had burned down one weekend. It hadn't."

"Why would she . . . you know, tell people I was in love with her?"

"Okay, I didn't want to get into it but how come you're going out with her all of a sudden?" Bobbi asked.

"She told me she thought her father was racist and we could find out by me calling him up and asking if . . . I could take her out." I was beginning to see a whole scenario. Caren hooked onto the race thing and now everybody was thinking we were a couple. "You think I've been had?"

"It happens when you're young," Bobbi said, opening her laptop. "You want to talk anymore about Sidney's problem? I think I have a solution."

Me, tearing my head back from Caren and getting it back on Sidney. "Go on."

"When we play next, Sidney is supposed to play Pullman," Bobbi said. "That's going to be a hard match. Suppose I get the coach to put him on the fourth board. That'll put him on a weaker player and he can relax a little. It's a bit of a comedown for Sidney but he's going to get his points anyway. This team is the last really hard one we're going to face this year until we reach the play-offs."

"Okay, but do you think Sidney will go for it?"

"He will if you talk him into it. You can tell him that it's to set up the play-offs," Bobbi said. "That'll put me up against Pullman, who'll probably beat me, but we might get a full three points out of the match if the two and three boards play well. If Sidney loses to Pullman in a quick game it'll blow morale and we might all lose. We just have to convince Sidney to go along with it."

That sounded good. I thought I could convince Sidney that it was best for the team and he'd go along with it. I told Bobbi that I would talk to him later.

I was on Wednesday schedule and had Language Arts and Physics to do after lunch. I couldn't think straight in Language Arts, and Physics could have been in Greek.

I couldn't believe that a seventh-grader had smoked me, but Caren had. It wouldn't have been so bad if she hadn't started telling everybody that I was in love with her.

In the hallway. There she was talking to Marie Castro. I went right up to her.

"Yo, Marie, mind taking a walk?" I asked.

Marie looked at Caren, giggled, and moved away.

"What are you going around telling people?" I started.

"Zander, don't hate me for loving you," Caren said. "Please don't say you hate me."

"I don't . . . I don't hate you or anything, but I just want to know what you're telling people," I said.

"Just the way I feel about you," Caren said. Her eyes were tearing up. "Can we talk about it Friday — *please?*"

"Yeah, I guess."

Caren smiled, turned, and started down the hall.

I wasn't sure if I had just set up a conversation for Friday or if I had just been had by a sneaky seventh-grader. Again.

Home. Mom had left a note on the television saying that there was food on the bottom shelf in the fridge and that she would be home late. I checked and saw two bags. One read SNACK and the other SUPPER. I opened them both. The snack was a sandwich: meatballs and peppers on a roll. The supper was an aluminum tray of fried chicken and yellow rice. I ate the chicken and rice first and then the sandwich.

I called Caren's house as I ate and her mother said she wasn't home.

"She's at band practice, but I'll tell her to call you as soon as she gets in," her mother said.

I started thinking about Sidney again and the Pullman kid. Lots of kids got pressured when they played ball, but I had never thought of kids getting pressured when they played chess. I felt sorry for Sidney but I felt even sorrier for the Pullman kid. He was good, he worked hard, but he wasn't being allowed to relax and just play.

Then I started thinking about LaShonda and Kambui and wondered if they felt any pressure to get good grades. Maybe that's why they liked the Cruisers, because we were kind of laid-back.

Finally, I started thinking about the kids that my uncle Guy had told us about. He hadn't given us any real details, just showed us the places they had died and then showed us how nice they looked when they had been alive. I knew that I couldn't just look at Sidney and see the pressure he was under to win all the time. I wouldn't have even thought of it if I hadn't seen the Pullman kid. I wondered if his father felt bad afterward. Probably not. He probably thought he was doing his son a favor by slapping him around.

I put on the television, then turned it off, then put it back on again. I was trying to think of a way to convince Sidney to play the fourth board. I went to the Internet and looked up what it meant to play which board. The way it looked was that the fourth board was the weakest on the team and I knew that it could be embarrassing for Sidney not to be first board. Where were all the easy answers?

I found his number on my cell and called him.

"Hey, Zander." Sidney.

"Hey, Sidney. Look, Bobbi wants to put you on fourth board against Thurgood Marshall. She said —"

"Whatever," Sidney interrupted.

"It's okay with you?"

"Yeah." Real quiet, though.

"You okay, man?"

"Yeah." Real quiet again.

"Yo, Sidney, is your head straight, man?"

"Yeah, I'm all good," he said.

He didn't sound *all good*. I told him I'd tell Bobbi that he was down for the switch.

I don't normally doubt the Cruisers. We are definitely chill in our approach to life and all up in the game, but Sidney and his whole world of chess was pushing me into corners I hadn't been to before, opening my eyes to pressures that you couldn't just walk away from. And the whole thing with the chessboard and Sidney's code meant that he was having trouble dealing with the program. It reminded me of the way I dealt or, I guess, didn't deal with my parents being split up. I didn't think chess could slip-slide into the world of just about violence. The Zander man tiptoeing down Wrong Street.

I knew everything wasn't okay at all, but I didn't want to push it. Sidney hadn't been convinced, he just took it. Maybe he felt we were putting him down. I wanted to call him back and say we weren't, but that might have felt like we were treating him differently, which we were in a way, and that might have made him feel . . . Where were the easy answers?

I called Bobbi and told her what happened. She said she would send the board assignments to Thurgood Marshall.

NO BID, SID!!!

Sidney Aronofsky, Da Vinci's lone hope for glory, has chosen to RUN AWAY from a match with Pullman in the upcoming chess match. We see Da Vinci's true colors as one yellow streak fading rapidly into the sunset!!!!

This was the flyer two girls from Pullman's school, Thurgood Marshall Academy, were handing out in front of our school at lunchtime. They had come all the way to our school to mess with us. I hoped that Sidney wouldn't see the flyer. He didn't have to. Mr. Culpepper saw it and called Sidney to the office. Then he called the Cruisers.

"No way!" he said. "Sidney is first board and he will remain first board. He is not a Cruiser and if this is your idea of how to dis-inspire our student body then I will go to Mrs. Maxwell and even beyond to see that your influence ceases once and for all! Do I make myself clear?"

"You're clear but you're wrong, sir," I said. "If Sidney doesn't want to play first board . . ."

"Sidney, what do you want to do?" Mr. Culpepper spoke softly but it was as if his voice was coming out all in capitals or something.

"I'd rather play fourth board," Sidney said, his voice hardly above a whisper.

I looked at Mr. Culpepper. He was turning red. Then a brighter red. Then he took several deep, slow breaths, held his breath for a minute, exhaled slowly, and said, "You may all leave my office now."

I felt real bad for Sidney. Kambui and LaShonda were telling him that he had done the right thing, and Bobbi was just looking kind of lost. I knew she felt bad. Our idea had been a good one, but the way Mr. Culpepper had put it, and the way the kids from Thurgood Marshall had put it, Sidney looked bad either way.

"You want to hang out after school?" I asked.

"No," Sidney replied.

"We meant to do the right thing," I said.

"I know."

I didn't have anything else to say and had to watch him leave with his head down.

CHAPTER TEN
Game Day

Going to a chess tournament is like going to an opera that's sung in a foreign language. You see everybody moving around but you don't really know what's going on. The game was at Da Vinci, and the Thurgood Marshall team arrived in a stretch limousine. No lie. The game was in the media center and there had to be a hundred kids from Marshall there to sit around and watch. The boards were set up in a semicircle near the windows. The blinds had been drawn and the windows shut to keep out the noise. The Marshall players took their seats first, and there was a murmur from the crowd. I looked up, but I didn't see anything going on.

"Pullman's on board four!" Cody Weinstein said.

They were putting their best player on the board that

Sidney was going to play. There was a brief discussion, and then Bobbi came over to me.

"Zander, they're switching to get at Sidney," she said. "They asked permission to make a change. If we say no it's going to be even worse than it looked."

"Where's Sidney?"

Bobbi looked around. "I thought I saw him down the hall," she said. "He was headed toward the bathroom."

I didn't know what to say.

At exactly four o'clock the signal was given, and the players started the clocks. Sidney was nowhere to be seen.

Pullman put his hands behind his head and leaned back in his chair. He was so pleased with himself that it was just dripping from him. There were webcams facing each board, and we could follow the games on laptops set up on the encyclopedia shelves.

Our players were concentrating on their boards. I looked over to where Mr. Culpepper sat, next to the computers. He was looking around the room, I guess wondering where Sidney was.

I imagined my friend outside looking for someplace

to buy drugs, and I felt so sorry for him. The games started moving along slowly, but still no Sidney. I knew his clock was running, and he would be having time pressure later on.

Bobbi looked over at me and then pointed toward the door. I turned and looked. I didn't see Sidney, but then I thought she must have meant for me to go look for him.

The hallway was empty except for a security guard reading a newspaper. The bathroom was near the end of the corridor. I went in and looked around. I was about to leave when I thought I heard a noise.

"Sidney?" I called.

"I can't come out."

"You stuck?"

"I just can't."

The door to the stall wasn't locked, but I didn't want to open it. I opened it anyway. Sidney was sitting on the john with his pants up.

"Hey, Sidney, I'm sorry," I said. "But I think you should come out. Go on in there and play the match."

"Zander, there's too much pressure."

"Yeah, I know, but the pressure is going to be there if you play or not, Sidney," I said. "It's going to be there for the next match and the next match. And if you don't play it's going to be there to make you play, because you've got the stuff and everybody knows that. So maybe you need to play and learn how to take the pressure off of yourself by not caring as much. Or maybe even caring as much but just giving yourself a break."

"You practice saying that, Zander?" Sidney asked. "You make it sound easy, but it doesn't work that way. Not for me, it doesn't."

"It worked for you once, man," I said. "Remember when you first met me, and some guys were all up in my face and trying to push me through a wall? You stood up for me even though you didn't know how to fight. You stood up for me even after they knocked your butt down. Go out there and stand up for yourself. Let yourself be knocked down again, but get back up. That's the Sidney I know."

"You think I should just say it doesn't matter?"

"No, try something like . . . it matters and I might get hurt but I'm doing what I think is . . . or might be . . . okay."

"Everybody is going to look at me when I come into the room," he said.

"Your clock is running," I said. "Pullman is sitting at their board four with a big grin on his face."

"Pullman?"

Sidney Aronofsky looked away for a moment, then stood up.

"Okay," he said, "let's get knocked down again."

I followed Sidney into the media center. He walked up to the board that Pullman was sitting at, glanced down at the pieces, and pushed his king's pawn two squares up.

Pullman instantly moved, and the next five moves went by so quickly I couldn't follow them. It was move! Hit the clock! Move! Hit the clock! Move! Sidney hadn't even sat down yet.

I saw Bobbi look over toward where Sidney and Pullman were playing. She nodded, then looked down at her own game.

Sidney sat and leaned forward. His hands were low between his knees, and he only moved them when he made a move. Pullman was leaning back in his chair and made me think of the old-time gunslingers in the Western movies.

Each player had his or her own style. Sidney had a slight head bob, and I imagined him working out the moves in his head. Todd was a seventh-grader with a narrow, muscular build, and he sat almost motionless. Bobbi rocked back and forth.

I followed Sidney's game until the fifth move as he and Pullman jockeyed for position. Then the game was over my head. I couldn't tell who was winning or if anybody was. The games went along quietly. No one made a sound. All of a sudden I could hear every noise that came from the street below. I tried to guess which of the vehicles were buses and which were trucks.

Then Sidney made a move, pushing a pawn with one stubby finger. Pullman smiled and reached for his piece. When his hand stopped in midair over the board and just *stayed* there I looked over at him. The smile was gone, and he was squinting slightly.

I glanced at Sidney. He looked the same, except that now his hands were above the board, and he was rubbing them together lightly. Pullman made his move, retreating his bishop, and Sidney instantly made another move.

Now it was Pullman rocking, then tapping his heels under his seat.

I didn't know how, or exactly what move did it, but I could see by their body language that the game had suddenly gone wrong for Pullman. He was twisting in his seat, hesitating as he reached for his pieces.

When he laid his king to one side, showing that he had conceded the game, his hand was actually trembling.

I felt sorry for Pullman, really sorry. As much as I wanted Sidney to win, I didn't want Pullman to lose and have to face his father.

Bobbi and Brendel won, too, and Todd got a draw. Da Vinci had won the match three and a half points to one half. Sweet.

"He was playing the Dragon Variation but he really doesn't know it!" Sidney was saying after Thurgood Marshall had left. "What was he *thinking*?"

"You back now?" LaShonda asked.

"On first board?" Sidney looked up at Bobbi. "Depends on what Bobbi wants."

"You're still first board," Bobbi said.

"I mean from checking out drugs?" LaShonda said.

"I think . . . I think I've got it together again." Sidney looked at LaShonda and his forehead wrinkled up. "It could go wrong, but I know I got some people on my side. That helps some."

"Just *some*?" LaShonda asked.

"Some," Sidney said.

THE PALETTE

The editors of *The Palette* want to offer our heartfelt congratulations to our own Sidney Aronofsky for his cool and heroic win over James Pullman in the recent chess match with Thurgood Marshall Academy. There had been some rather shoddy comments about Sidney prior to the match, but Sidney met the comments and the challenge of the contest with his usual coolness and dignity. Pullman once again went to the King's Gambit, which Sidney had declined in their previous meetings. This time Sidney accepted the offered pawn and went on to play a masterful and aggressive game. Overall, Da Vinci won the match with three wins and a draw. Way to go, team!

— *Ashley Schmidt*

CHAPTER ELEVEN

As the World Turns!

It's great going out with people you don't particularly like," Mom was saying as she inspected me from the bathroom door. "That way if the date goes wrong you won't feel bad."

"You ever go out with somebody you didn't like?" I asked.

"Your father."

"You didn't like him?"

"Not when I first went out with him," Mom said. "I thought he was a nerd."

"He is."

"But then I fell in love with him, and we got married."

"Just like that?"

"No, there was a lot of kissing and hugging in between the first date and the marriage," Mom said. "You want me to tell you about that?"

"No!"

I had just about decided to call Caren Culpepper and tell her I couldn't make the date, but Mom had convinced me not to. She said it wasn't any big deal for me, but it might really hurt Caren to break the date at the last minute.

Caren had said she wanted to talk to me when we were in school, and I didn't mind talking to her except I couldn't think of anything she would say that I could find interesting. She had also asked me not to hate her for falling in love with me, and I didn't want to hear anything about no love. What I needed to do was to take Caren out, be reasonably nice to her, and let her down easy.

Mr. Culpepper lived in a great pad on Waverly Place down in the Village, a block from where they sell the best and cheapest hot dogs in the city. The plan was to snatch Caren up, take her uptown to a movie on 23rd Street, buy one bag of popcorn, dig the flick, walk her home, and say "The End."

Knock on the door. Mrs. Culpepper opened it. She's pretty in a schoolteacher sort of way, with everything in place and a nice smile. She invited me in, even though I would rather have waited in the hallway. Mr. Culpepper came into the kitchen. He was wearing a long-sleeved shirt with rolled-up sleeves and a sweater vest. That must be his idea of casual, which made me smile.

"Is there something humorous happening, Mr. Scott?"

"I never saw you with your sleeves rolled up before," I said.

"It's not exactly appropriate for school," he said. The rolled-up sleeves were Waverly Place, but the voice was still Da Vinci.

Caren came out wearing a shimmering pink dress, black leggings, low black heels, and a beret. She looked okay.

"I trust I will see you two before the clock strikes and we're all turned into mice and pumpkins," Mr. Culpepper said.

"You'll see us," I said.

"So, how are you doing?" Caren asked as we went down in the elevator.

"Okay," I said. "How are you doing?"

"I'm all good," she answered.

Caren is not that tough-looking but she dressed up nice. She was looking pretty good, and I couldn't think of anything to say. We copped the F train at West 4th and four minutes later we were on 23rd.

"Look, Caren, you know we can't be, like . . ."

"Like what?" She took my arm.

I hadn't expected her to take my arm or anything like that. I looked at her, and she had this big smile on her face, which kind of threw me off. I had wanted to tell her that we couldn't be serious or anything like that, but she had the kind of smile that put you off.

Got to the movie, bought the tickets, and found seats. I forgot the popcorn and asked if she wanted some. She said no. I wanted some, but I didn't go get a bag just for me. We were waiting for the movie to start and she put her hand under my wrist and held my hand from the inside. Right away I knew she had moves. I didn't know where she got them from, but mama had some moves.

The movie started, and she looked straight ahead. I was wishing I had some popcorn so I could get my hand free, because she was definitely holding on.

The movie was about some woman who had dreams about what was going to happen to people and all the dreams came true. It was pretty nice. There could have been more violence in it, though. If the girl had a dream about someone dying, they would just get sick and die, nothing outstanding.

But through the whole movie Caren was holding my hand, and when things got tense on the screen she held it even tighter. Finally, the movie was over. I thought that she was liking this too much, and I needed to put some reality back into the scene.

"Let's walk to my house," she said.

"Yeah, okay," I said.

"You think I look all right tonight?"

"You usually look pretty dumpy," I said.

"What looks dumpy?"

"You wear those jeans with the sequins and stuff."

"I didn't know you were noticing me that much," she said.

"I wasn't." I stopped and looked at her. Caren was about five foot five, so she was looking up at me and she was smiling, and I was wondering if she was actually falling in love with me or something. I didn't think people fell in love that easy, but she was only in the seventh grade so I thought maybe she had.

So we walked down Sixth Avenue and she had my hand again, and I didn't want to tell her to just let it go because I didn't want to be mean or anything like that, but then I wondered if she thought I was going to kiss her good night.

"What are you thinking?" she asked. "You're so quiet."

"I was wondering what you were thinking," I said.

"I'm just liking being with you," she said.

We got to Waverly Place and I asked her if she needed me to go upstairs with her. She said yes.

We got into the elevator, and she leaned against me and put an arm around my waist.

The elevator stopped at her floor. We walked toward her door. She stopped and lifted her face toward me.

I didn't want to kiss Caren Culpepper, and I didn't want to look stupid like I'm afraid to kiss a girl, so I kind of leaned down a little and she came up a little and we kissed. Just as the door opened.

Monday morning. Math finally ended and I was on my way to World History when Kambui and LaShonda grabbed me in the hallway.

"Emergency meeting!" Kambui said in this dramatic whisper. He pulled me into Mr. Goldstein's empty Typing class. We saw Bobbi, and LaShonda frantically waved her over.

Bobbi was out of breath when she got to us. "What's up?" she asked.

I was thinking that, at the least, Sidney got arrested again over the weekend. Maybe he even died of an overdose.

"Zander, the whole seventh grade is talking about you and Caren going out Friday night, and how you were all over her!" LaShonda said.

"She said that her father caught you messing with her in the hallway," Kambui said. "That true?"

"Man . . ."

"She said you were squeezing her hand so hard in the movie she was almost crying!" LaShonda said.

"Man . . ."

"She called me over the weekend and wanted me to tell you that you and her are through," Bobbi said. "She said she wanted to save herself for marriage."

"Man . . ."

FROM THE DIARY OF ALEXANDER SCOTT

Dear Diary,

Where are the headlines? The whole world is turning upside down every other minute and there's nothing about it in the papers. One minute my man Sidney is depressed and acting like a stone-cold addict, and the next he's a thousand miles away from drugs and back to kicking rump on the chessboard. Where were the headlines about that? And how come nobody writes about how rough a game of chess can be? One minute Jamie Pullman is all world, and the next minute he's being slapped around by his father. Where were the headlines about that? I think it's the little stuff going on that pushes the big stuff onto the front page. Ashley asked me to put some words together for The Palette, but what I'm thinking is that I need to learn more about what's shaking before I throw it into the oven. The real deal lies somewhere between what you see on the front pages and the way some people are living their lives.

I can't get the pictures that Uncle Guy showed us out of my mind. No way. I guess they weren't important enough to make the news, but they were people, kids just like the ones going to Da Vinci, or Powell, or Boys and Girls. All they are now are a few pictures left for the world to see and somebody's pain. That is so foul.

And how about that Japanese model who got too skinny to work because she wanted the job so bad and you have to be skinny to look good?

And yo, diary, what's up with Caren? One minute I don't want to see her because she's not even near to being hot, and then I go out with her and she's looking kind of hot and I don't like her but I do like her in a way, but just when I decide that I need to drop a dime and tell her that we aren't happening she tells the world that we're not happening because I'm Wolfman chasing her in the moonlight or whatever.

Hey, diary, is the world spinning faster than I can think, or is the whole life thing a Big Secret and we're only dealing with our little corner of it? How come I don't have the real deal figured out yet? What's up with that?????

CRACKING THE CODE

Here's how to decipher the hidden chessboard message that appears on page 78.

All sixty-four squares that appear on the chessboard are part of the code. Use the code-cracking grid below. Each chessboard square has five numbers. Find the first two numbers in the vertical column of the grid. Find the next three numbers in the horizontal column of the grid. Then find where the vertical numbers intersect with the horizontal numbers to locate the corresponding letter. These letters spell out Sidney's message.

	000	001	010	100	110	111
00	A	B	C	D	E	F
01	G	H	I	J	K	L
10	M	N	O	P	Q	R
11	S	T	U	V	W	XYZ

COMING UP NEXT . . .

THE THIRD BOOK IN THE NEWS CREW SERIES

A STAR IS BORN

Now it's LaShonda's turn in the spotlight, where she's forced to consider what's more important — worldwide fame and adulation or loyalty to her autistic brother. To find out whether LaShonda gets a standing ovation or the curtain pulled down on her, read the next book in the News Crew series. Meanwhile, here's a peek at some coming attractions from that book.

A STAR IS BORN

You can't do that, LaShonda Powell!" Mr. Culpepper was already turning a fifth shade of red. "There will be NO nudity involved with any students from Da Vinci!"

"Then you better cancel the whole performance!" LaShonda was getting up close and personal, and Kambui was trying to get in between them.

"This is . . . this is . . . the chance of a lifetime, young lady. . . ." Our assistant principal was beginning to sputter and Kambui was practically dragging LaShonda out of the door.

Bobbi McCall was in tears. Yes, tough-as-nails Bobbi was on the verge of a major boo-hoo.

"What's going on?" I asked Bobbi in the hallway. "I thought LaShonda was doing great?"

"She was," Bobbi said. "Until they told her that if she took the scholarship they would have to separate her from her brother. No way she's doing that, Zander. And the Cruisers have to back her up!"

I knew the play we were going to put on would put the Cruisers on the map big-time, especially with all the noise about LaShonda's costumes. But if we blew it after all the press coverage they wouldn't be able to dig a hole deep enough for us to crawl in!

When some community activists wanted to do away with Da Vinci for being "too elitist," the principal, Mrs. Maxwell, called a town meeting to discuss the school. Part of the meeting was a play written by the Cruisers based on Romeo and Juliet. But the hit of the play was the costumes — part Elizabethan and part Electric Grunge — designed by LaShonda. The New York Times called them "stunning!"

Now LaShonda wants to ditch the whole concept?

WALTER DEAN MYERS (1937–2014) was the 2012–2013 National Ambassador for Young People's Literature. He was the critically acclaimed *New York Times* bestselling author of nearly one hundred books for children and young adults. His award-winning body of work includes *Somewhere in the Darkness*, *Slam!*, and *Monster*. Mr. Myers received two Newbery Honor medals, five Coretta Scott King Author Awards, and three National Book Award Finalist citations. In addition, he was the winner of the first Michael L. Printz Award.